RETRIEVAL

THE RETRIEVAL DUET (BOOK 1)

ALY MARTINEZ

I proposed on our first date.

She laughed and told me I was insane. Less than a day later, she said yes.

It was a whirlwind, but we were happy…

Until we got greedy and wanted a family.

It was a life I couldn't give her, not for lack of trying. Fertility just wasn't on our side. We sought out doctors and treatments. Spent money we didn't have. Lied to our families. Smiled for our friends. Put on a brave face for a world that didn't understand.

Finally, we were successful…

Until we were forced to bury our son.

We were left broken, battered, and destroyed.

They say love is in the details, but it was the details that ruined us.

This is the story of how I took back what had always been mine.

The *retrieval* of *my* wife and *our* family.

RETRIEVAL
Copyright © 2016 Aly Martinez

ISBN-13:978-1537352213
ISBN-10:1537352210

All rights reserved. No part of this novel may be reproduced, distributed, or transmitted without written permission from the author except for the use of brief quotations in a book review. This eBook is licensed for your personal enjoyment only. If you would like to share this book with others please purchase a copy for each person. This eBook may not be re-sold or given away to other people.

RETRIEVAL is a work of fiction. All names, characters, places, and occurrences are the product of the author's imagination. Any resemblance to any persons, living or dead, events, or locations is purely coincidental.

Cover Designer: Hang Le
Photograph: Eric Battershell
Models: Tessi Conquest and Burton Hughes

Editors: Erin Noelle and Mickey Reed
Proofreader: Julie Deaton

Formatting by Champagne Formats

RETRIEVAL

PROLOGUE

ROMAN

The house was dark when I quietly twisted the lock so as not to wake her. God knows she needed the sleep. I didn't know how she still functioned when her days were filled with tears and her nights weren't much better. It was precisely the reason I stayed gone as much as I did. Or so I'd thought as I'd thrown myself into work. Money couldn't solve my problems, but it might have been able to solve hers.

My body ached, and my lids barely stayed open despite the pot of coffee I'd downed not even an hour earlier. It was a miracle I had been able to drive at all. I should have just crashed at the office, but after yet another failed prototype, I'd needed an escape.

Instead, I'd gone home—the very place I'd spent so many nights trying to avoid.

Only one foot was over the threshold when I suddenly

froze.

"Elisabeth?" I called, flipping the overhead light on.

My shoulders fell as I found her sitting on the sofa, her long, blond hair curtaining her face and suitcases surrounding her feet.

"What's going on?" I asked as my gut wrenched, already knowing the answer.

I had no right to be surprised. I'd all but forced her hand. If I was honest with myself, it was what I'd wanted—for her. However, none of that made the pain of reality any less agonizing.

My heart raced. "Elisabeth?" I prompted again, needing to hear her say the words almost as much as I dreaded it.

"I can't stay here anymore," she whispered at the floor.

Acid rose in my throat.

Out of habit, I dropped my keys into the basket she'd bought when we'd first moved in. *"If you fail the key basket, the key basket will fail you,"* she'd announced with an infectious smile the day we had become homeowners to the two-bedroom-two-bath starter home we could barely afford. It was just seconds before I'd swept her off her feet and made love to her on the hardwood floor of our foyer in the middle of the day.

But such was life as a newlywed.

Inside that house with her was the only place I'd ever wanted to be.

Until the fantasy of forever had worn off and the walls of real life had closed in on us. Once my refuge, our home became an inescapable prison with bars built of my failures.

I couldn't breathe inside that house any more than I

could look her in the eye.

We'd only been married for five years. But, seeing her now, I felt like it'd been a lifetime since I'd peered into her eyes, promising to love her in sickness and in health.

But it wasn't like she was the same woman, either.

Over the last six months, she'd wasted away both physically and mentally in front of my eyes.

And I'd done absolutely nothing to help her.

But how do you throw a lifeline when you yourself don't even have a rope to hold on to? I might have been able to keep her afloat for another day, but I'd never have been able to pull her back to me.

We merely existed on the same plane. Living under the same roof, eating meals at the same table, sleeping in the same bed. But we were far from sharing our lives together.

"Are you coming back?" I asked, not willing to accept the truth that lingered in the air around us.

Her deep-green eyes lifted to mine—the red rims and the dark circles doing nothing to hinder her beauty. Swallowing hard, she shifted her gaze to the mantel on the other side of the room. I knew what she was looking at, but I refused to follow her into the past.

That might have been our biggest problem of all.

She was still living there.

And I refused to go back.

"Elisabeth?" My voice softened, but the question remained the same. "Are you coming back?"

"No," she replied, swiping the tears from her cheeks.

A thousand arrows fell from the sky, searing into my soul. My breath hitched, and my lungs burned. This was it—

the end of my life as I knew it. But, in that moment, with her shoulders hunched forward in defeat, I realized that it was the end of hers, too.

Why did that realization hurt more than the lifetime of loneliness that was awaiting me when the sun rose?

I lifted a hand and rubbed my chest, hoping to ease the mounting pressure threatening to overtake me. "Don't do this," I mumbled through the pain.

I wasn't sure who I'd meant that for though.

Was I chastising myself for having asked her to prolong the inevitable just because I wasn't ready to lose her yet? Or was I asking her to stay in this sham of a marriage for even one day longer?

Probably both.

"You'll be okay," she assured me, pushing to her feet and gathering her bag, complete with our Yorkie, Loretta, tucked in her mesh dog carrier.

My pulse quickened, nature's fight-or-flight finally kicking in. But I'd been in flight mode for entirely too long. There was no fight left.

I stepped into her path. "Elisabeth, please." I wasn't sure why I kept saying her name. I secretly hoped that it would snap her out of it, bringing her back to the reality of it all. But it was the reality that was killing us.

"I'll take off work tomorrow," I pleaded. "We can talk. Figure things out."

It was selfish. Completely and utterly selfish. But that was nothing new for me.

Her chin quivered as a steady stream of tears fell from her eyes. "Promise me something, Roman."

I would have promised her the entire fucking universe if it had made her stay one night longer. But who was I kidding?

We were over.

We both knew it.

"Anything," I whispered, reaching down to take her hand, desperate for the connection I didn't deserve.

"Remember to live." Her voice caught, and a silent sob tore through her.

Cupping the back of her head, I pulled her into my chest.

"I can fix this," I swore, but it was yet another lie. "We just need time."

Her shoulders shook as she cried in my arms. "We…we promised. We told him we'd live for him."

I closed my lids and clung to her tighter.

We were supposed to be fighting and screaming. That was what soon-to-be-divorced couples did. But that wasn't us. We didn't hate each other. Elisabeth was my soul mate on every level.

And she was paying the price for that.

Minutes later, the tears stopped and she backed out of my arms. I fought the urge to regain my hold, forcing her to stay. But her sad resolve as she hurried to the mantel and then to the door made it clear it'd be a wasted effort.

Never in a million years had I thought I'd be standing there, watching her walk away.

But, then again, I'd never expected her to have the urn of our only child cradled in her arm, either. A reminder of just how much I hadn't been able to give her. How much I'd *never* be able to give her.

My past, present, and future were walking out of my life, and I stood immobile as every fiber in my being screamed for me to drop to my knees and beg her to stay.

To take her in my arms and tell her that we'd figure it out.

To reclaim my life once and for all.

But how would that have helped *her*?

Staying wouldn't magically bring back her smile. Nor would it make her look at me with those bright-green eyes that made me feel as though I could conquer the world.

It wouldn't give me back the crazy woman who argued with her whole heart and loved with her entire soul. No. Those days were gone.

I'd lost that woman somewhere in the bitterness between grief and blame.

We'd been happy once.

But we'd gotten greedy and tried to start a family.

That was her future. Not mine. Regardless how desperately I longed to give it to her...and then selfishly take it for myself.

Sex. That's how babies are made. Children as young as elementary school are taught the simple biological facts of reproduction.

But what they never tell you is that, for one in six couples, having a baby goes a little differently.

For Elisabeth and me, it looked more like this:

Thirty-six months of crushing disappointment.

Three miscarriages.

Hundreds of tests our insurance company refused to cover because the inability to reproduce was not considered a health condition.

Countless tears.

Helplessness.

Failure.

Failure.

Failure.

Her broken heart.

My empty chest.

Thirty-seven thousand dollars we didn't have.

In vitro fertilization.

A sperm donor.

A handful of hope.

A positive pregnancy test.

Five months of utter bliss.

Earth-shattering devastation.

A funeral for a child I would never get to see grow up.

A job that became my only reprieve from reality.

And now…losing the only woman I would ever love.

I'd always been amazed by how much punishment a heart could take. I was broken, battered, and destroyed. And yet, much to my dismay, as I watched the front door close behind her, my heart kept beating.

CHAPTER ONE

ELISABETH

Two years later...

"Where are you taking me?" I laughed as Jon blindly guided me through the empty house.

His tall body pressed against my back while his callused hand covered my eyes.

"Promise me you won't freak," he said cautiously.

My body stiffened. "What did you do?" I fought against his grip, no longer willing to play his game.

He squeezed my hip to keep me in place then muttered, "Chill. And promise me."

"I will make no such promises. If you have to tell me not to freak, chances are I'm going to flip."

He chuckled. "You totally are."

I nudged an elbow back into his ribs. "This is not funny."

A grunt left his mouth, but it was followed by more laughter, which made it known that he disagreed.

Even with my objections, he continued to lead me through the carpeted rooms until my high heels clicked against tile.

"Okay." He paused. "It's not a big deal. So no more elbows. I can't hazard a broken rib. I've got work to do today."

I huffed, unwilling to agree for fear of making him a promise I couldn't keep. "Just get it over with already."

"Exactly what every man wants to hear," he teased and then dropped his hand.

I gasped, covering my mouth as I spun in a circle, taking in the newly renovated bathroom. "Oh my God. You… you did this?" I asked, moving toward the double vanity. "You did this?" I glided my fingertips over the smooth edge of the brand-new marble countertop.

He shoved his large hands into the pockets of his dirty jeans and shrugged. "You were never going to sell it with laminate countertops, Liz."

My mouth fell open when I saw the dual heads in the new shower, where a linen closet had been not even a week ago. "And a new shower?" I breathed, opening the door and stepping inside.

He smiled, leaning his shoulder against the wall and crossing his work boots at the ankle. "And a new shower," he confirmed.

I did a three-sixty and shrank when I saw the custom tile work I knew for certain he'd done with his own hands. "I…I can't pay you for this."

His deep-brown eyes narrowed. "I didn't ask you to."

"Jon," I murmured as I caught sight of the new molding butting up against the resurfaced ceiling.

His eyes followed mine. "Ah…I may have gotten carried away. But you know I can't half-ass a job. It's the eleventh commandment."

I shook my head, relief filling my chest at the same time guilt took up root in my stomach.

I'd been trying to sell that house for nearly six months, and with every passing week, it was costing me more and more to carry. I was barely keeping my books in the black as it was.

While my meager commissions as a realtor paid my monthly bills, they weren't enough to cover this place. If I wanted to continue flipping houses, I needed to get out from under it as quickly as possible. I'd dumped my life savings into that four-thousand-square-foot skeleton. And then, when that had run out, I'd taken out a loan from the bank and maxed out all of my credit cards.

It still wasn't enough.

I'd vastly underestimated how much it would cost to get that old Victorian back to something inhabitable—much less desirable.

As it stood, if I could get it sold, I'd be able to recoup my investments and possibly walk away with a few grand in my pocket to show for my hard work.

But, as appealing as the profits were, that wasn't why I loved spending my evenings covered in dust, working on whatever project I'd gotten in my head the day before. There was something about watching that house come alive around me that gave me a satisfaction I hadn't felt in years.

But, like most things in my life, I'd taken on too much too quickly.

I did the very best I could on my own, but I was only one person. As I'd learned from the fiasco while removing the fiberglass insulation, I wasn't necessarily qualified in all areas. Luckily, a friend of mine had put me in touch with Jon Hartley when I'd told her that I needed a contractor. He was a godsend who'd agreed to cut me a deal as long as he could work after five every night.

We'd quickly become friends, and his hourly wage had soon converted to beer and home-cooked meals.

He was fresh from a divorce and using any excuse to keep from going home to an empty house.

I understood him all too well. I was two years out and using one empty house to avoid another.

Jon and I had spent many nights in that old house together. But, in all of our time together, never once had any lines been crossed.

However, looking around at what had to be at least a ten-thousand-dollar bathroom renovation, I was starting to worry Jon's lines of friendship were slightly different than mine.

"Say something," he urged, walking over and then stopping directly in front of me. He wasn't touching me, but there was a certain intimacy at his proximity.

I sucked in a deep breath and swayed away in order to crane my head back. "This is too much. What the hell were you thinking?" I whispered.

"Honestly?" he asked softly. The corners of his mouth tipped up in a half smile that should have melted me. There was no denying that he was a good-looking man. But…he was *Jon*.

I bit my lip, praying for lies. I didn't want honesty. Not from him. Not about this.

"Jon," I breathed.

His hand found my hip and gave it a tight squeeze. "I was hoping that, if you sold this place, I could finally get some sleep."

I smiled, exhaling on a rush. But, when his eyes landed on my mouth, I felt no relief.

His other hand came up to my face, his thumb trailing back and forth across my cheek as he held my gaze. "And I was hoping, if you sold this place, you'd finally let me take you out and spend some time with you that doesn't require power tools."

I swallowed hard. *Shit. Damn.*

"You did this so you could ask me out?" I nervously toyed with my skirt. "That's an expensive bouquet of flowers."

He grinned. "You need out of this place, Elisabeth. And I'm not just talking the financials." Dipping his head forward, he brushed his nose with mine. "You're hiding."

"So are you," I countered, but my voice was weak.

"I was in the beginning. But, now, I only come back because of you." His lips swept mine, but I didn't reciprocate.

I wanted to though. Or, more accurately, I *wanted* to *want* to.

Jon was a good man. He'd slowly become my best friend over the last six months. And isn't that the foundation of a strong relationship? God knows that's not how it had been with Roman. And look where that had gotten us.

With Roman, he'd proposed approximately five hours into our first date. I laughed and told him he was insane. But those silver-blue eyes and that wicked grin made me breathless for the first time in my life. Our relationship was based on an overwhelming desire and an unexplainable need for one another.

It had been nearly two years since we'd last spoken, and I still felt the invisible strings binding us together. I couldn't explain my pull to that man any more than I could explain why I didn't feel it with Jon.

But maybe this was exactly what I needed. Something new and fresh but without the risk of the all-consuming kind of love I'd felt for Roman.

It didn't have to be like that with Jon. Hell, it had taken him months to even ask me out.

This was different.

Different could be good.

I *needed* different.

"Okay," I murmured, opening my lids with a newfound resolve.

"Okay?" A mixture of relief and hope danced in his gaze.

"Okay, I won't freak out about the bathroom." I paused and shyly glanced to the side. "And okay, I'll let you take me out."

A wide, white smile split his mouth. "Okay, then."

I abruptly stepped away from him and lifted a single finger in the air. "But! I'm paying you back for this."

"I don't want your money. I was trying to do—"

"No arguments. When I sell the house, I'm paying you back. I hope you kept receipts."

He smirked. "I thought you said you weren't going to freak out?"

"Yeah, well, I changed my mind. And you better agree to my caveat before I change my mind about you taking me to dinner at Harper's, too."

His tipped his head, his lips twitching as he asked, "Harper's?"

I motioned a hand around the bathroom. "You can't ask a girl out with a ten-thousand-dollar bathroom and not expect to take her to a fancy restaurant for dinner. That would be false advertising. You've set the bar. Now, let's hope you live up to it."

He laughed, shaking his head. "Harper's it is, then. And it wasn't ten grand, but I'll let you pay me back for the materials *only*." He pointed over my shoulder. "Except for the shower. That's my gift to you."

I smiled and extended a hand in his direction. "Deal."

He stared at my hand for several seconds before clapping it and giving it a hard tug, dragging me in for a hug.

It was nice. His arms wrapped around me, securing me against his hard body as he stroked up and down my back.

So nice that I momentarily lamented the fact that I felt absolutely nothing in return.

It was just past seven when I got home from the old Victorian. Jon and I had stayed working on the guest bathroom that now looked like a hellhole compared to the master. Jesus, I couldn't believe he'd pulled that renovation off while I'd been out of town. I also couldn't believe I'd agreed to go on a date with him.

Shaking my head at myself, I tossed my keys in the basket and shut the front door. Loretta came barreling into the room as fast as her tiny legs would carry her.

"Hey, crazy girl," I cooed, bending down to give her the attention she demanded. It was rare that I went to the other house without her, but we'd just gotten back from a trip to Virginia to see my parents. "Oh, don't look at me like that. After an eight-hour car ride, we both needed a little space." I smoothed the short, gray hairs on the top of her head down.

She licked my face then wiggled from my arms. I put her back on the floor, and she immediately pranced to the back door, watching me over her shoulder the whole way.

"All right. All right. Go play," I said, sliding the back door open.

She'd missed her freedom while we'd been staying at my parents' place. It backed up to a lake, and I was terrified she'd get busy chasing one of the ducks, fall in, and drown. Poor pooch hadn't gotten a single minute off the leash over the last week.

After closing the back door, I began sifting through the stack of mail.

Bill. Bill. Bill. Advertisement. Chain letter?

I knew this because it had the words *chain letter* in handwritten block letters on the back of the envelope.

I smiled to myself as I ripped it open.

Dear Elisabeth,

I don't normally believe in things like this, but it's true! You must call your sister within the next thirty minutes or you will experience seven years of bad luck. Nancy Smith received this letter and she simply threw it away. The very next day, her hymen grew back, her cat ran away, and she slipped and fell in her bathroom.

Don't be like Nancy. Call your sister.

<3 Kristen

I didn't have a sister. And sure as hell not one as crazy as Kristen. But for the five years Roman and I had been married, I'd had her as a sister-in-law. I was an only child with parents who lived over five hundred miles away, Roman's family had become my own. His parents had been amazing, welcoming me into their lives with open arms. Never once had I felt like anything but their blood. But I'd lost them all the day I'd walked away from him.

It'd been weird not having them in my life at first, but a clean break was what we'd all needed. Or at least it was what *I'd* needed—starting anew without the memories of the past hanging over my head with every step.

For the first six months after our divorce, I couldn't stomach restaurants he and I used to frequent, much less keep a relationship with his family as they all carried on with their lives—with him.

However, the Leblanc family was a force to be reckoned with. His mom and his sister flat-out refused to accept the brush-off. In the beginning, they called daily, and when I didn't answer, they took to showing up at my house with wine and sushi. If I'm being honest, they were the only reason I made it through that first year.

As time passed, they slowly gave me my space, recognizing that moving on would probably involve another man. It hadn't. At least, not yet. Though, considering my date with Jon, that might be changing.

I reread her letter and settled on one of the wooden barstools that surrounded my large, granite island. It was a custom build—a gift from my parents when we'd first closed on our tiny starter house. I'd never forget the shock on Roman's face when the contractor had accidentally left the bill. My parents weren't loaded by any stretch, but I'd been born to them late in life, long after they'd given up the hopes of having children.

My father had spoiled the hell out of me when I was growing up. Fortunately—and unfortunately, depending on at what age you'd asked me—my mom was strict as hell, so I hadn't grown up to be a little shit. My father had been wrapped around my finger before I'd even come out of the womb, so when I was twenty-six years old, marrying a West Point graduate, Army Captain, and all-around amazing man, Daddy went over the top.

I swear I thought his smile would swallow his face as he placed my hand in Roman's on our wedding day. A day that had two hundred guests, a full dinner, an open bar, and an equally ridiculous price tag attached to it. But his little miracle only got married once, he'd said.

She apparently only got divorced once, too.

Fighting with my mind to stay grounded in the present,

I grabbed the phone and dialed Kristen while I finished going through the stack of mail.

More bills. More junk mail. A Christmas card from an overachieving client seeing as we were still two weeks from Thanksgiving. And then my body jerked as I lifted a letter from Leblanc Industries into my sights. My face flashed hot as ice formed in my veins.

I was tearing it open just as Kristen answered.

"You're alive!" she greeted enthusiastically.

"Son of a bitch," I snarled through clenched teeth as I pulled a check from the envelope.

"Shit. Did your hymen really grow back? I should have known better than to try my hand at the chain mail game."

"Your. Brother," was all I had to say.

She cursed under her breath. "What did Mr. Personality do now?"

Loretta began yipping at the back door, but I ignored her demands and headed straight for the fridge.

"Um…hello. What did Roman do?" Kristen called when I didn't immediately reply.

But I needed to get at least half of a bottle of wine in my system for this chat.

"I'm drinking," I explained.

She sighed, knowing exactly what that meant. "Shit. How much?"

I didn't bother with a glass. Instead, I yanked the cork out with my teeth and then drank directly from the bottle.

"More than the last one?" she asked when I didn't reply.

"Mmmhmm," I mumbled around the bottle.

She groaned. "Dad talked to him. I swear. We've *all*

talked to him. He doesn't listen."

I swallowed the mouthful of Chardonnay, making a mental note that wine should *never* be chugged. But that didn't stop me from tipping it up once again.

Kristen waited patiently on the other end of the phone until I'd finished enough to gather my thoughts. I sucked in a deep breath, silently cursing myself for having given up the meditation bullshit I'd started when we were trying to get pregnant.

When I finally got my emotions under control, I very calmly opened my mouth and then yelled at the top of my lungs, "He doesn't listen to anyone!"

So much for under control.

"I know," she replied somberly. "How much?"

"Two hundred thousand dollars."

"Fucking shit," she whispered.

I dug through my fridge, praying that a mini bottle of wine had gotten lost somewhere in the back behind the mass amounts of Tupperware filled with leftovers. I still hadn't mastered the art of cooking for one. A stray beer from God knows when was all I found, but I quickly twisted the top off and chugged it. Beggars can't be choosers on the hunt for intoxication in order not to kill your ex-husband.

"This has got to stop!" I said, slamming the beer on the counter. Foam bubbled from the top. "Shit. Shit. Shit!" I rushed to the sink, making it just in time to keep it from spilling.

"You okay?" she asked.

I ignored the question. I was in no way okay. I was, however, pissed off, and she was the only one around to listen. "I don't want his money. I didn't get a say when he paid off the house. But I'll be damned if I'm taking quarterly payouts."

She was quiet for a minute. And I knew what was coming. It was the same bullshit his mom had spewed when I'd first called to ask her to make him stop sending me checks over a year ago.

"He's trying to take care of you," Kristen whispered.

I barked a humorless laugh as angry tears pooled in my eyes. "Don't you dare feed me that crap. You know better than anyone that he could have taken care of me when we were married. Now, he's lost that right."

She sighed. "He started the company when y'all were still married. Technically, half of it should be yours."

"Technically?" I snapped, squeezing my eyes shut and gripping the phone so tight I feared it would break. "You want to talk technically, Kristen? Because, *technically*, Roman started that little shithole company less than twenty-four hours after Tripp died. *And, technically*, he ignored me for six months to get it up and running when I needed him the most. *Technically*, I was grief-stricken and still went back to work three weeks postpartum so he could quit his job and play scientist. *Technically*, that fucking company ruined my entire life. So, you know what? *Technically*, I don't want shit from Rubicon, Leblanc Industries, and, most of all, Roman." I stopped to catch my breath when a sob tore through me.

"Jesus Christ," she breathed.

"Just make it stop," I choked out. "It's been two *years*. Make. Him. Stop."

"Okay. Okay. Calm down. I'll talk to him again. I'll

make Mom and Dad give it another go, too."

My hands shook as I pinched the bridge of my nose. "I'm trying to move on with my life, but I swear to God he won't fucking let me."

"You're right," she replied immediately, probably fearing another explosion. "I'll take care of it. I'll make it stop."

I swallowed hard and did my best to collect myself only to give up and polish the foamy beer off instead. "Thank you," I grumbled, tossing the bottle and the check into the trash can on my way to the back door to let Loretta back in. "And I'm sorry. I didn't mean to call you just to bitch about your brother."

"It's okay if you did, ya know. We all know he's a prick. It's not a newsflash. Besides, I miss you, and if you're only willing to call and bitch, I'll take what I can get."

A small smile played on my lips. "You know, I should have married you instead."

"Damn straight. I'm a freaking catch. It's a shame neither one of us swings that way."

The anxiety slowly ebbed from my system, and my smile grew. "Definitely a shame."

"Okay, now that we got the 'Roman is an asshole' out of our systems, what's new with you?"

God, I've missed Kristen.

I toyed with the ends of my hair and then mumbled, "Jon asked me on a date."

"What!" she shrieked so loud I had to pull the phone away from my ear. "Oh my God. What did you say?"

I sank down onto the stool and kicked my heels off. "I said, 'Okay.'"

CHAPTER TWO

ROMAN

It was past seven when I'd last checked the clock. Still at the damn office, I was beyond fed up with my so-called "meeting." With every intention of ending the bullshit once and for all, I extended my hand across my desk.

"I'm sorry to hear that."

Simon Wells, the seventy-something-year-old founding CEO of Defender Armor, stared blankly at my proffered hand. "Mr. Leblanc—"

A slow grin grew on my lips. "Simon, I believe we're way past the formalities. Please, call me Roman." I pushed my hand farther across my desk and leveled him with a menacing glare. "Then get the fuck out of my office."

His gaze jumped to mine, the corners of his eyes crinkling as they narrowed. "I'll repeat: This is my final offer."

It always was.

We'd been doing this song and dance for nearly two

years. Ever since my team had created the most superior bulletproof material on the market. Rubicon, named due to its natural red coloring, was not only stronger than the competition but half the weight and thickness, making it easier to wear for long periods of time and conceal under uniforms during covert operations. In the last year, it had become the most sought-after product in the business.

I knew it.

And so did Simon Wells.

Which was precisely why he was sitting in my office for the tenth time in so many months, attempting to buy a bulk order at less than half of its current asking price.

Done with the games, I dropped my hand and stood from my chair. After fastening the top button on my suit coat, I strolled away while casually shoving a hand into the pocket of my slacks. I stopped at the door and gave him my full attention. "I hope to God this is your final offer, Simon. Because, if you come back with a number that low again, you may want to consider wearing some Rubicon of your own." Arching an eyebrow, I dared him to argue.

I should have known better. Simon lacked the ability to quit. It was annoying as fuck when you were across the table from him, but I suspected it was what kept his company on top for the last decade.

The muscles in his jaw ticked as he remained in his chair. "Cops are dying out there," he seethed through his clenched teeth.

I shrugged. "Yes. They are. Because they're wearing *your* vests. Maybe you should do something about that."

His fist slammed down on my desk as he shot to his

feet. "You bastard! Have you no conscience? I know for a fact you made a deal with the military for half of what I'm offering." His hand shook as he raked it through his gray hair. "Sign the fucking contracts and let those officers dying on the streets go home to their families."

I tipped my head to the side but otherwise remained impassive. "And how exactly would you know what the bottom line on my contract with the military read?"

He squared his shoulders and attempted to regain his composure. A flicker of pride hit his eyes as he assumed he'd guessed correctly. "I'm not stupid, Leblanc. Word gets around."

He wasn't wrong. The body armor community was small.

For nearly fifty years, Kevlar had dominated the market. But, as new weapons and ammunition capable of penetrating the material began flooding our battlefields—and then, eventually, our streets—it was time for a change. Always the entrepreneur, I saw the literal and figurative gaping hole in the industry and pounced.

I wasn't a scientist though, and I quickly found myself nose-to-nose with the same brick wall most of the country was facing. Companies were pouring millions into research, knowing that the pot of gold at the end of the race was going to be astronomical.

I didn't have millions, but what I did have was a life I refused to face, a marriage I was hiding from, and the idea that dollar bills could fix it all. I threw myself into research, took a few investors on, and then hired the best team of scientists I could afford: two ex-cons with MIT degrees and my old Army NCO, who had been struggling to find a job in the civilian sector.

It wasn't exactly ideal.

But maybe that's why we were successful.

Desperation was one hell of a motivator.

For months, the four of us spent every waking moment huddled together in a makeshift lab, running on cheap coffee and fueled by hopes and dreams. Research was extensive, and failures were a daily occurrence.

Too heavy.

Too thick.

Too bulky.

Until Rubicon.

One day, I woke up miserable, alone, and broke.

The next, I woke up miserable, alone, and in the running for *Time* magazine's man of the year.

In a matter of months of going live with our product, Leblanc Industries had revolutionized the entire market—if not the world.

And it was exactly why Mr. Wells was beating my door down in order to save his own business. People weren't buying his second-rate products anymore, and as the days passed, Defender Armor fell deeper and deeper into the hole.

Now, he was hoping I could save his ass.

But I'd never been known as a philanthropist.

And his idle threats only served to piss me off.

He had no fucking clue what he was talking about when it came to my sales. Because, if he did, he'd have known that I sold Rubicon to the military for a quarter of what he was offering me. But the difference was the military wasn't using my product in flak jackets and then selling it at four times what they'd paid, which was exactly what Wells was planning to do.

The Army was using it to save lives. If I hadn't had employees who needed to be paid, I would have given it to the government at cost. I'd watched too many good soldiers die during my time in service not to want our men and women equipped with the very best. I would have loved to arm our police forces with it as well, but that did not mean giving my product away so another company could profit from it.

Unfortunately, I didn't have the facility readily available to make the body armor. And Wells didn't have my product. We were at a stalemate.

He couldn't afford me. And I couldn't go at it alone—at least, not yet.

The good news for me was that Rubicon had dozens of other uses that kept our bank accounts overflowing. And, as far as I knew, bulletproof vests were a rather niche market.

He needed me far more than I'd ever need him.

"This is ludicrous!" Wells growled.

I nodded matter-of-factly. "I agree. Now, get the hell out and don't come back unless you're ready to sign *my* contracts. No revisions."

His eyes burned into me as he finally moved toward the door, pausing just before leaving. "You know, I expected more from you. Former soldier, now CEO. I love a rags-to-riches story just as much as the next guy. It does the whole world well to be reminded that hard work pays off. But then there are men like you who disgrace us all by allowing the money and power to go to your head. It'd do you well to remember where you came from, because if you keep this up, I have a feeling you'll be back in that dingy garage lab sooner than you think."

My lips thinned, but I took a step forward, once again extending my hand for a shake. "Then perhaps it's good that I'll have you to save me a spot in the unemployment line."

The vein in his forehead bulged as he nearly vibrated with anger. "You—"

Turning, I gave him my back and strolled back to my desk. "Have a good day, Simon."

Moments later, the door to my office slammed and my whole body sagged.

"Jesus. Fucking. Christ."

The intercom on my phone buzzed immediately. "Mr. Leblanc, your sister is on line one. She's been calling for the last hour and says it's important."

Fucking great. I loved my sister, but Kristen had exactly two speeds in our relationship: bitch *at* me or bitch *to* me. And, considering we'd had dinner the night before and she'd bitched *to* me for nearly three hours about a dickhead she'd slept with and then he hadn't returned her calls, I figured her calling with something important meant I was going to get bitched *at*.

I groaned, preparing for whatever shitstorm she was about to drop at my feet.

"What's up, Kit-Kat?" I asked, after lifting the receiver to my ear.

"Oh, don't you dare 'Kit-Kat' me."

Yep. Bitch-at-me mode.

I switched the phone to my other ear and wedged it against my shoulder as I fired my computer up. "I'm seriously not in the mood to take your shit tonight. I've had an old man up my ass all fucking day. I really don't need you joining him."

"I just got off the phone with Elisabeth. She's getting remarried."

My body solidified, causing the phone to fall from my ear. Scrambling after it, I ignored the way my chest constricted.

I reminded myself that it was what I'd always wanted for her—to find someone who made her happy and could give her the things I never could. I just hadn't considered how much it'd hurt when it finally happened.

Slowly lifting the phone back to my ear, I licked my lips and opened my mouth, but not a single word escaped.

"Roman?" she probed.

I cleared my throat, strapping on the false bravado. "Good for her. This is important to me how?"

"You have to stop sending her checks. Her fiancé is livid about it."

Now, that made me smile. "Sounds like a personal problem. That money is hers. If her man has a problem with her past, I'd be happy to have a talk with him. Set him straight." Before I killed him.

I swear I heard her roll her eyes from across the line.

"Right," she said. "Just what every woman wants. The new guy having a chat with the old guy. *Especially* when the old guy is still in love with you."

"I'm *not* still in love with her," I growled. That would

imply I'd ever been *out* of love with her. "And this is not my problem. So, if that's all you called to say, I need to get back to work." *Or, more likely, down a bottle of scotch.*

"Damn it, Roman. Okay. I lied. She's not getting remarried. After the shit you pulled, I'm doubting she ever will."

The second sucker-punch hit me square in the gut. I hated the idea of Elisabeth actually moving on with someone new, but I hated the idea of her being alone even more.

"Excuse me?" I bit out. "The shit *I* pulled? She left *me*. So get off your high horse and get to the point where I'm supposed to care right now. I'm not doing anything wrong by sending her money that is rightfully and legally hers."

"It's not legally hers! You made *certain* of that."

That I did. And I'd never forget the agonizing pain on her face when I'd told her that, in exchange for her fifty percent of Leblanc Industries, she could keep everything else.

The house.

The furniture.

The cars.

The dog.

Tripp.

She had gotten our entire lives.

I'd walked away with a suitcase—and the yet-to-be-developed Rubicon.

"Yeah, well…I'm feeling generous. Besides, judging by that piece of shit she's still driving, she needs it."

"Aaaand…how the hell do you know what she drives?"

Because I've driven by our old house enough times over the last two years to wear potholes in the roads. "I saw it parked at the cemetery the other day."

She gasped. "You went to the cemetery?"

"For fuck's sake, don't sound so surprised. He was my son."

"Was he? Because, if I remember correctly, when she finally buried the urn last winter, you were nowhere to be found."

"I was working!" I defended. It was a lie. But there was no way I was copping to what I'd really been doing that day. Not even to my sister.

"You're always working, Roman! I had to make an appointment with your secretary a month ago so we could have dinner last night."

"Okay, so now you're bitching at me because I work too much?"

She drew in a sharp breath and then demanded, "Stop with the checks. She's finally getting her shit back together, and you're just making it harder. I swear to God, if you ever loved her, then you'll stop this bullshit right now. You signed the divorce papers two years ago, Roman. Let. Her. Go."

I closed my eyes and rubbed my temples. She was right, but it ate a hole through my soul to think about Elisabeth wanting for anything. Wife or not. Just because our marriage hadn't worked out didn't mean I didn't still care about her. But there was only so much I could do. I'd lucked out and been able to pay the house off, but only because she hadn't been able to afford to remove me from the deed yet. Short of dropping briefcases of cash on her porch, my options were limited.

I wasn't stupid. I knew she hadn't cashed any of the checks I'd mailed her. But there was a level of comfort in knowing that the next one was in the mail. She hated me, and she was stubborn as hell. But she was at least reasonable. If she got desperate, she'd swallow her pride and cash it. And that knowledge was the only reason I slept at night.

"I'll consider it," I lied.

"You'll consider it?" she yelled. "There's nothing to consider, Roman. Stop sending her the checks!"

I shook my head and pushed back from my desk. "Look, I need to go. See what you can do about getting her to cash that last one and I'll consider stopping."

"She's not gonna cash—"

"Then *convince* her," I ordered, standing up and digging my wallet and keys from my desk drawer. "She's shit at selling houses. I looked it up—she only sold four last year. Her specialty is interior design, not real estate. If I know her at all, she probably treats them like puppies and falls in love with each house, refusing to sell them to owners she deems unfit. Kit, she needs that money. We both know it."

She was silent for several beats, and then she let out a groan of frustration. "Were you dropped as a child?"

I grinned, knowing I'd won. Kristen was quite possibly the only person in the world who could convince Elisabeth to accept money from me. Hell, if Kristen got her mind set on it, she could negotiate world peace. The woman was pushy as shit. I credited my skills in negotiating business deals to having grown up with her. We hadn't had conversations around the dinner table—we'd had debates. And, judging by the ease in which she'd given in during this little spat, it meant she had agreed that I should have been sending Elisabeth that money before she'd even called.

"No more than you were," I smarted back.

"Shit. Maybe that's our problem," she whispered.

"Could be. Now, I *really* need to go. We'll talk soon."

"Yeah. Yeah. Yeah. I'll probably talk to your secretary first."

I shoved a hand in my pocket and smirked. "Probably."

CHAPTER THREE

CLARE

"About time you showed up," Luke said, spinning in his chair as I walked into the gym with Tessa on my hip. I peeked over my shoulder at the childcare room. "Yeah…uh…please tell me there's someone in there still."

"Yes, ma'am," he drawled, moving around the counter.

"Thank God," I breathed, my shoulders drooping in relief. "Sorry I'm late. I…um…lost track of time." I swallowed hard, fighting to keep the emotion out of my voice.

It was bad enough that my eyes were bloodshot from crying. I couldn't hide that any more than I could the gash in my hairline being held together with three butterfly bandages, but the last thing I wanted was to talk about it, so I needed to at least sound okay.

The gym was my escape. I hated working out as much as the next girl, but it was the only place I was able to erase the rest of my fucked-up life.

Tessa lunged from my arms, diving toward Luke.

He eagerly caught her and poked her belly, blowing a raspberry against her cheek. He was so good with her. Too good, probably.

I gently pulled her back into my arms and smoothed her blond curls down as I avoided his gaze. "Do you still have time for me tonight? I mean…I can always reschedule. Maybe I'll just work on cardio. I could use some time—"

He interrupted my rambling with a loud laugh. "Nope. Not happening. Give it up now, Clare. You're not getting out of leg day."

"Right. Leg day," I mumbled under my breath.

My whole body ached, my ribs were screaming just from holding Tessa, and the bruises on my thighs were probably already purple, but I would have spent my entire life doing legs if it meant I didn't have to go home.

My chin quivered as I finally looked up into his kind eyes.

He was almost successful in hiding his flinch. He sucked in a hard breath and blew it out on a curse. "Jesus, Clare," he whispered, aiming a comforting hand at my shoulder.

I ducked out of his reach. The gym might have been my sanctuary, but I wasn't free there. Someone was watching me.

Always watching.

"Legs. We should probably get started," I squeaked.

His handsome face hardened as he crossed his thick arms over his chest. "Maybe we should go to my office and go over your meal plan instead."

I shook my head and wiped a stray tear off my cheek

with my shoulder. "We just made a new meal plan last week. It's leg day, Luke." I curved my lips up in something I hoped would pass as a smile. "We do legs on leg day."

The muscles on his jaw ticked as he stared at me, pity filling his eyes until he finally relented, raking a hand through his dark-blond hair. "Son of a bitch." He tipped his chin toward the childcare door. "Go. Get her settled. I'll meet you over at the mats."

Luke had been my personal trainer for three months, and in that time, he'd learned the gig. I could tell it killed him each time I came into the gym with fresh injuries or tear-stained cheeks. But he kept his opinions to himself and read between the lines, never pressuring me to spill my guts but asking just enough questions to remind me that decent people existed.

He was an incredibly nice guy. And, in another life, I would have even gone so far as to say he was sexy, too. But I didn't live in a world where I was allowed to focus on anything but keeping myself alive and my daughter safe. He was only filling in for Cindy until she got back from maternity leave. And, truthfully, Walt probably already wanted to kill him just for having contact with me, but I'd have done whatever I had to in order to keep him off my husband's radar. And that included leg day.

Walt was insistent that I keep myself in shape, but he hated when I spent too much time outside the house.

And he really hated it when I took Tessa with me.

I'd always thought he feared that, if I had her with me, I might never come back.

And he would have been absolutely correct.

There was nothing I wouldn't have done to get away from him.

Anything except actually leaving.

I'd tried that twice. And the scars of those nights still covered my body, both inside and out.

Turning him in to the police wasn't an option, either, though. He'd made sure I had more than enough of his sludge on my hands to put me away for life.

And then where would that have left Tessa? Alone with a monster.

I'd never wanted children with Walt, but he had been adamant that we start a family. And, as his wife, it had been my duty to provide him with one.

I'd cried month after month when those pregnancy tests had come back negative—they were tears of joy. I hated my life, and the thought of forcing an innocent child to join me in Hell seemed like a tragedy.

Unfortunately, Walt took our problems to the professionals.

I'd never forget how numb I felt as a reproductive endocrinologist smiled at me from across the desk, promising he'd help us.

I sobbed, hoping he couldn't.

After a round of in vitro fertilization, in which two embryos were transferred into my uterus, I prayed harder than ever before that it wouldn't take.

But I guessed God wasn't taking requests that day.

Nine months later, we welcomed Tessa into our lives.

It wasn't fair to her. But I'd have done it all over again. That little girl saved my life.

And, no matter how long it would take me, I'd find a way to save hers.

After dropping Tessa off, I stiffly made my way over to the mats.

"Change of plans. It's arm day," Luke announced.

I winced, lowering myself to the mat. "I appreciate the concern. But I assure you legs would be easier."

He frowned and then cracked his neck. "Okay. Then measurements. We haven't done your measurements yet this week. Let's go to my office and—"

"Enough!" I hissed. There were so few things within my control. I'd be damned if working out wasn't one of them. "It's fucking leg day, Luke. Can we *please* just stretch and get started?"

He blinked but otherwise remained unfazed by my outburst—until he whispered, "Clare…"

I spread my legs, folded over to one side, pressing my nose as close to my knee as my aching body would allow, and changed the subject. "I was sore yesterday. I should have taken Sunday off. Maybe we can implement yoga back into my workouts."

"Let me help you," he whispered, but we both knew he wasn't talking about stretches.

I barked a laugh. It felt just as hollow as it sounded. "I don't need a friend, Luke."

I needed a friend more than words could adequately express. But I wasn't going to find it in a personal trainer who had no idea what the hell he was getting into. And I sure as hell wasn't going to stand by while he fell down the rabbit hole trying to rescue me.

"Please. Do us both a favor and mind your own business."

The muscles at the base of his neck strained, but very slowly, he lowered himself to the mat beside me and began stretching, too.

Then he watched for over an hour as I cried through most of our workout.

It hurt like hell, but the most painful part was knowing that, when it ended, I'd be forced to get Tessa and head back home.

———◈◇◈———

"There she is," he said as I pulled Tessa from her highchair.

I froze and set her back down, my entire body going on alert at the deep rumble of his voice.

He wasn't supposed to be there. His BMW wasn't in the driveway when I'd gotten home from the gym. And I hadn't heard him come in. Which meant he'd been in the house the whole time. *Oh God, what did I do that he could have seen?*

The fact that I hadn't known he'd been there sent chills down my spine. My job, as a mother, was to keep Tessa safe, and the biggest part of that was knowing where *he* was at all times.

I closed my eyes and sucked in a deep breath. My chin quivered as I plastered on a brave smile that had long since become the only one I possessed anymore.

"Hey," I whispered, turning to face him.

His green eyes lit as they landed on me, raking down my body and up again.

I'd changed after I'd gotten home. And not into the baggy T-shirt and worn-out pajamas I craved. I kept those hidden in the back of my drawer for when he was out of town. If Walter was home, I had to put effort into how I looked. Hair, makeup, jewelry. There was no such thing as comfort or lounging. He'd settle for nothing but perfection, and after our showdown earlier that afternoon, I couldn't risk pissing him off again. Not while Tessa was awake.

After my shower, in which my baby girl had pulled every toiletry I owned out of the cabinets, I'd tugged on a tight pair of white pants that accentuated my butt and a pink-and-white silk blouse I knew he loved. I'd donned the diamonds he'd given me at dinner on our one-year anniversary—not to be confused with the ones he had given me the next morning as an apology for having beaten me out of consciousness because he'd thought I had been flirting with the waiter. Though he often requested that set specifically. A quiet reminder. As though I could ever forget.

"Jesus, your face," he breathed, striding toward me.

Walter Noir was handsome. There was no denying that. I'd thought I was the luckiest girl in the world after he had seductively slid his business card across the counter at the seedy diner I'd been waitressing at when we'd first met. He'd been wearing a fitted, black suit that cost more than my car and a smile so beautiful that it hurt to look at. With his dark hair, green eyes, and olive skin, I was awestruck immediately. He was captivating in every sense.

Seven years later, I was the captive one, he struck more often than not, and the hurt was now in *my* smile.

"It's okay," I replied as he lazily stroked his thumb over

the cut on my eyebrow.

He nodded in agreement then pressed his lips to my forehead and murmured, "How was the gym?"

I fought back a gag as he let the kiss linger while sliding his hands down my sides and over my ass.

"Great," I managed to squeak.

Thankfully, he stepped away, and my breath silently rushed out on a relieved sigh—until I realized where he was headed.

"Come here, baby girl," he said, stepping toward Tessa.

Panic ricocheted in my chest.

When Tessa had been a baby, she'd loved her father. And, by all accounts, he'd loved her, too. He was kind and attentive, worrying over her every peep. It was the same way he had been with me while we'd been dating. However, I knew love could turn into something ugly with Walt.

After all, he'd loved me once, too.

He had never once laid a hand on his daughter, though he'd hit me in front of her enough that she feared him all the same.

Over the last six months, things had changed with Tessa. She'd turned two and become aware of the world around her. That world being one where her father was an extremely dangerous man.

The crying any time he picked her up had started shortly after her birthday, and it infuriated Walt to the point that I spent my nights wondering how much longer she'd be safe under the same roof with him. I'd die before I let him hurt her, and as the days passed, I feared that might just be what it would come to. Time was running out. There was only so long that I could blame her reaction to him on teething or whatever mystery illness I could come up with.

"Mama," she cried, reaching out for me with both arms as he approached.

My pulse spiked as I stepped into his path.

"Can I talk to you for a minute?" I tried to distract him by placing my hands on the lean muscles of his pecs and pressing myself against his front.

He arched a menacing eyebrow. "Can I say hello to my daughter first?"

I stood on my toes and ghosted my lips across his. "Well, you could, but she skipped her nap today, so she's in a terrible mood. How about I put our girl to bed then properly apologize to you for this afternoon?"

His eyes heated as his fingers painfully gripped my hips. "What do you have in mind?"

With shaky hands, I reached behind me and took Tessa's tiny outstretched arm. She calmed instantly, so I kept my attention on Walt and seductively purred, "I'd rather hear what *you* have in mind."

He studied my face for a moment, his eyes inspecting the bruises I'd done my best to conceal with makeup. "You know, if you'd asked that question earlier, you wouldn't look like this."

"I know. Which is why I'm asking now."

He held my gaze for a minute longer then murmured against my mouth, "Get her in bed. I have a few calls to make first."

I nodded swiftly, jumping in surprise when he squeezed my ass.

He lifted his focus over my shoulder and cooed, "Night-night, princess." Then he turned his eyes back on me. "I won't be long. Go take a shower."

I'd taken a shower less than two hours ago. But that was the one thing Walt and I agreed on—I couldn't get clean enough. Not when his filth clung to me.

I kept the smile up as he left the room. Then, when he was out of sight, I sucked in a ragged breath and tamped down the overwhelming desire to vomit.

There was no time for that.

I had but one objective: keep Tessa safe.

I'd sacrifice my heart, my body, and my soul to accomplish it.

Tonight, it was my body.

CHAPTER FOUR

ELISABETH

I awoke the next morning to my phone screaming on my nightstand. Or maybe it was only ringing, but my head was splitting in half from the sound.

"Shit," I groaned when the night before came flooding back to me. I slapped my hand around until I found the offending device.

I answered only to silence it.

"Mrs. Leblanc?" the man on the other end questioned.

I threw my arm over my face and sighed. "It's Keller now, but yes, this is she."

"Oh…sorry about that. *Ms. Keller.* My name is Detective Rorke, and I'm with the Atlanta PD. I was wondering if you would be able to come by the station today and answer some questions we have for you."

"Me? You want to question me? I mean… I'm sorry. What kind of questions?"

He chuckled. "I'm sure it's nothing. Could you be here in an hour?"

An hour sure as hell didn't sound like it was nothing.

I slowly sat up, allowing my head time to adjust to being vertical again. "Uh...can you at least tell me what it's in regard to?"

"I'd rather we discuss this in person."

"In an hour? Right."

"As soon as you can get here, Ms. Leblanc," he added kindly.

"Keller," I corrected then sighed. "I'll be there as soon as I can."

"Perfect. See you soon."

As he hung up, I jumped out of bed and rushed to the shower.

I shouldn't have rushed.

Three hours later, I was still sitting in an empty hallway at the police station, no closer to finding out why I'd been brought in than I had been on the phone.

When I'd arrived, Detective Rorke hadn't been there, so a uniformed officer escorted me to a room that screamed *Law & Order* more than it did a friendly chat.

Staring at myself in what I was positive was a two-way mirror, I racked my brain for what they could possibly need to question me about. With not so much as a speeding ticket on my record, I was a rule-follower by nature. Trouble and I did not coexist.

After about an hour, a different officer came in and escorted me to a chair in the hallway. More than once over the last two hours, I'd stopped people walking by, trying to get to the bottom of why I was there. But, each time, I'd been shut down by a tight smile and some variation of, "I'm sure it's nothing."

But, as my eyes lifted and I saw Roman *fucking* Leblanc entering the mouth of the hallway, flanked by two men in suits, I knew it was definitely *something*.

I hadn't seen him in the two years since the divorce, but it could have been a thousand years and I wouldn't have forgotten him.

However, with that said, I didn't exactly recognize this man, either.

The man I'd fallen in love with didn't parade around at ten a.m. on a Thursday morning in a suit. Hell, my Roman had argued about wearing one to his own wedding. Regardless of where we had been heading, fast food or a funeral, you wouldn't have caught him in anything but jeans, a T-shirt, and a tattered ball cap.

This guy, though, was wearing that power suit as if it had been custom-made for him. Which, judging by the way it hugged his every muscular curve, it probably had been.

I narrowed my eyes as he strode down the long hallway. It was definitely him, but not even the posture matched the man I'd vowed my life to. My Roman smiled with his whole body and could charm a popsicle from a toddler with nothing more than a wink. He was approachable, funny, laid-back, and gorgeous beyond all belief.

As I raked my eyes over him, I realized that, much to my dismay, the gorgeous part had remained intact, even if the hard set of his jaw and the resolute square of his shoulders tarnished it.

Power and money swirled in the air around him with every step.

I shouldn't have been surprised. I knew he was successful now.

I'd seen the magazine covers.

I'd heard our old friends talking.

I'd received his checks.

This was the new Roman, and it was so fucking wrong that my heart went into mourning all over again.

Suddenly, his silver eyes landed on me and, with a whoosh, the air became too thick to breathe. It was okay because my breath was trapped in my lungs, unable to escape around the newly formed lump in my throat.

He blinked for several seconds. Then his shoulders relaxed and the façade dissolved, leaving the man I had fallen in love with beautifully exposed in front of me.

The hairs on the back of my neck prickled the same way they had when we'd first met.

Back then, I'd mistaken it for love at first sight.

Now, I took it as a warning.

"Why are you here?" I accused in a low voice.

Cocking his head to the side, he returned, "Why are *you* here?"

His words hypnotically washed over me. He'd always had that effect on me. No matter how wound up I'd get, Roman could calm me with nothing more than a touch or a whisper.

Until the day he'd abandoned me.

I focused on that memory as I shot back, "I have no clue. But I'm starting to think it's probably your fault."

The corner of his lips twitched in the most annoying—and sexy—way possible. He pressed his left hand to his chest and feigned, "My fault?"

My mouth dried as the ache in my chest clawed up my throat.

His ring finger was bare.

It wasn't as though I'd expected him to be wearing his wedding ring after all this time. It was just that I'd never seen him without it. I'd given Roman that cheap gold band twenty-four hours after we'd met, when we'd gotten married at the courthouse without telling a single friend or family member.

He never took it off.

Never.

He'd still been wearing it as he'd walked out of the courtroom the day our divorce was finalized.

I swallowed hard and dropped my gaze to the floor. I couldn't do this. Not today. Maybe not ever. There was a reason I'd left him. This shit shouldn't still hurt.

And yet, it did. Agonizingly so.

"Yes, your fault," I whispered, but there was no resolve in my voice even to my own ears.

Following my lead, he gentled his voice. "I have no clue why I'm here. And, quite honestly, I'm more confused now that you're here, Lissy."

The familiar nickname made my head snap up.

As a woman with the name Elisabeth, I had no less than a dozen nicknames. Beth, Liz, Ellie, Biz, Lizzy, Bee, Elle… I'd had them all over the years. Friends, family, people I'd just met—they all abbreviated my name.

But the difference was that Roman pronounced the S.

"I'll take that," Roman said, snatching my driver's license from my hand after I'd been carded for wine on our first date. "Elisabeth with an S, huh?" He smiled, causing my heart to nearly pound out of my chest.

My cheeks must have flashed a million shades of pink, because his smile grew.

I nodded. "My parents wanted to make absolutely sure I never got one of those personalized pencils at the elementary school book fair. They're evil people like that." I shrugged. "Mission accomplished."

He blinked at me for several seconds, sporting the most breathtaking grin I'd ever experienced. Then, finally, he reached across the table and took my hand. There weren't sparks the way they flourished in romance novels or movies.

No. What I felt when Roman Leblanc took my hand was more than any poet, author, or screenwriter could describe.

It was the culmination of every emotion I'd ever experienced. The high of happy, the depths of sad, and the spine-tingling chill of ecstasy.

He continued grinning at me as my world flashed from black and white to screaming color all around me.

Then he smirked and replied, "They sound horrible, Lissy."

Not Lizzy.

Lissy.

I'd lived twenty-six years of life before that night.

But, suddenly, I was alive for the very first time.

I knew absolutely nothing about that man.

But I knew he was mine.
And I was meant to be his.

As I snapped back to the present, anger spiraled through my veins. "Don't call me that," I hissed.

He shoved his hands into the pockets of his pants and rocked forward on his toes, but he issued no apology. He just stood there arrogantly grinning at me.

Such was life with Roman Leblanc.

And, as it turned out, life *without* Roman Leblanc, too.

"Mr. and Mrs. Leblanc," a man's voice called from the end of the hall.

Roman and I both looked in the direction as an older man with salt-and-pepper hair and a Santa Claus belly approached. "I'm Detective Rorke. I apologize for your wait, Mrs.—"

"Ms. Keller," I corrected before he had the chance to go any farther. Standing in the hall with Roman was bad enough without someone else joining him in his little name game from the past.

"Right. Sorry," he said, turning sideways in order to slide past Roman. "Let's move in here." He opened the door to the room I'd originally been in before they'd relocated me to the hall.

I stood and waited for Roman and his legal entourage to enter the small room, but he swept an arm in a grand gesture for me to go first.

Always the fucking gentleman.

I rolled my eyes and walked inside. Though I did it with attitude, so flounce might be more accurate.

I heard Roman's deep throaty chuckle as I passed.

I wanted to give him hell, but more than that, I wanted this to be over with. So I kept my mouth closed and settled in a metal folding chair on one side of the table, being sure to give the chair next to me a hard shove, scooting it to the end farthest away.

Roman didn't react, but I was positive he'd noticed.

"I see you brought your lawyers, Mr. Leblanc," Rorke stated, opening a manila folder like he had all the time in the world.

Roman crossed his arms over his chest. "I was called to a police station with two hours' notice. For questioning in a matter I wasn't informed about. You'll have to excuse my caution." Judging by his tone, he didn't want to be excused at all.

What I took from that exchange was that Roman got two hours' notice. Meanwhile, I had barely been able to speed-shower, choke a bagel down, let Loretta out, and then apply makeup in the rear-view mirror on the way over.

I secretly hated him even more.

Rorke nodded, but he didn't seem placated. "Innocent men rarely travel with *two* attorneys," he said, poking the beast.

Roman's eyes darkened as his face turned to stone. "Good cops rarely drag innocent people in for questioning without allowing them time to find proper representation." His eyes pointedly flashed down to me then back to Rorke. "So, yes, I do travel with two attorneys, but now, I only have *one*. Mr. Kaplin is with me and Mr. Whitman will now be representing Elisabeth *Keller*." He spat my last name, but that wasn't what caused me to jerk in my chair.

"What? No, he's not. I don't need *representation*." And I sure as hell didn't need to be billed whatever hourly wage allowed Mr. Whitman to buy that expensive—albeit stylish and well-fitted—suit.

"Shut it, Lis," Roman snapped, never dragging his eyes off Rorke.

Oh. Hell. No.

I snapped right back, "You did not just tell me to shut it."

Roman continued his stare-down with the detective as he called out, "Whit, advise your client."

Whit inched over to me. "Don't say anything. I'll answer all questions for you."

"You will *not*!" I replied. "We just met. You don't *know* the answers."

He arched a challenging eyebrow and dragged a chair over to sit next to me. Then he shot me a cocky grin and said, "I know the law, which means, in this room, I know *all* the answers."

My mouth fell open, and I glanced back up at Roman.

He smirked at me, and I'll be damned if that didn't cause an unwanted, but very real, flutter in my stomach. *Shit!*

"I *don't* need an attorney," I informed the entire room.

"Well, now, you have one in case you do," Roman returned.

"I don't *need* an attorney, *Roman*."

His lips thinned as he scowled. "Well, now, you *have* one in case you do, *Lissy*."

I clenched my teeth and ground out, "Stop calling me

that."

Vaguely, I heard Detective Rorke clear his throat, but just as quickly, Roman's hand went up in the air, snapping to silence him. Then, bending at the waist, my ex-husband leaned down until he was only inches from my face and growled, "Sure thing, *Lissy*."

Yes. *Growled*. Like some sort of man-cub raised by a pack of bears.

So, clearly, I had to ask, "Did you just growl?"

The muscles on his jaw ticked as he righted himself and focused on the ceiling, muttering, "Jesus fucking Christ."

That wasn't an answer, so I pushed. "Did you *seriously* just growl at me?"

He groaned and lowered his gaze to mine, stating incredulously, "You're at a police station for questioning. I offered you a lawyer. God forbid."

My chair protested against the tile floor as I pushed away from the table and up to my feet. "I don't *want* or *need* a lawyer. I haven't done anything wrong." I was moving toward him when I suddenly remembered that we were, in fact, in the middle of a police station with at least three other people looking on—maybe more if you counted whoever could be on the other side of the two-way mirror.

Shit.

Iced by my good manners, I sucked in a calming breath. "What I do *want* is to get whatever mess you created over with so I can go home."

Roman barked a laugh. "Aaand…we're back to this being my fault."

Rorke took that moment to join our conversation. "Nobody needs a lawyer."

All eyes swung to him.

"At least, not yet," he finished. "Now, if you two will *please* just sit down and shut up, I'll explain why I asked you to come down today."

CHAPTER FIVE

ROMAN

Elisabeth Keller.

Fucking Keller.

There were no words to convey how I'd felt when I'd seen her sitting in that hallway. Time had frozen with a single glance.

She appeared tired, too thin, and her hair was still damp on the ends, which caused it to frizz out in a way I knew she hated. But, even with all of that, she was still the most beautiful woman I'd ever laid eyes on. However, that probably had more to do with the fact that she was in my veins than it did her actual appearance. But I'd never, not once, seen Elisabeth with just my eyes. My heart was just as much a part of the way I viewed her as my retinas.

And still, after all this time, my body reacted to her the same way it always had—full alert.

Atlanta was a big city, but in the last two years, I'd never seen her once. And, in the beginning, I'd tried to accidental-ly-on-purpose run into her more times than I'd ever admit.

Of all the places to find her, a hallway at Atlanta PD was the one location I'd never considered.

Elisabeth Keller's idea of trouble was pocketing extra packets of sugar at the coffee shop. And, even then, she would have felt guilty, tossed and turned all night, and then promptly returned them the next day.

But there she sat, all wide-eyed innocence staring at me as though she were the one seeing an oasis in the middle of the desert.

Though, as far as I was concerned, she was the mirage. A woman I needed more than water and yet couldn't reach no matter how hard I tried—at least, not anymore.

Then she had to go and catch an attitude with me. It should have pissed me off. She had no right to come out of the gate swinging, blaming me for trouble that didn't exist. But, the moment she let loose, it only made me nostalgic.

It was that same attitude that had made me fall in love with Elisabeth approximately one hour into our first date.

"They sound horrible, Lissy," I said after a story about her parents. It was a joke, but her entire face lit.

And, with just one glance, it lit something inside me, too.

I'd wanted to strip her naked when she'd opened her front door, but it wasn't until we were at dinner that I knew I'd face the wrath of a thousand gods just to make her smile.

And worse, I'd burn the world around us in order to keep it aimed at me.

I was lost in her eyes when the server asked if we were

ready to order.

I quickly said yes.

She quickly said no.

She adorably narrowed her eyes.

I cocked my head and smirked.

Then I made the grave mistake of ordering for her.

My innocent angel disappeared, but the independent woman on the other side dug her hooks into me even deeper.

Using her menu to block her mouth from the waiter's view, she whisper-yelled, "I'm not eating chicken parmesan!"

"You said it sounded good a minute ago," I defended.

Her chin lifted, and she flashed her eyes around the restaurant. "It did at the time, but you have no idea how I eat it!" Again with the angry whispering.

I loved that she was standing her ground. But I especially loved that she was so obviously mortified that she was doing it in the middle of an Olive Garden, where people might possibly overhear her—including the waiter, who was watching our chat with subtle entertainment.

Mine wasn't so subtle. Therefore, I smiled huge and asked, "There's more than one way to eat chicken parmesan?"

"There is for me." She nodded confidently then tucked her long, blond hair behind her ear.

God, she was beautiful.

I sat back in my chair and stared as something inside me broke. I was twenty-seven years old. I'd had my fair share of dates and women, but not one of them had held my interest for any length of time. However, for some inexplicable reason, in a matter of minutes, I knew I wanted to argue with Elisabeth—with an S—Keller about chicken parmesan for the rest of my life.

"Oh, please, enlighten me, then," I teased.

She rolled her eyes then once again glanced around us, surveying our possible audience. "That's a second-date meal," she hissed. "Tonight, I'll have the soup and salad."

I twisted my lips. "That's it?"

"That's it," she confirmed.

I looked up at the waiter. "She'll have the chicken parmesan. Bring it out every possible way a person can order it. Pull up another table if need be."

"Roman, no!" She slapped at my arm, but I caught her hand and intertwined our fingers.

I held her gaze until the waiter walked away, at which point I seductively whispered, "Lissy, yes."

Her cheeks flushed, and then she gave me the innocent angel back. Her eyes darted to our hands before shyly sliding away. "That's a ton of food. And trust me, I'm a whack-a-doo. They'll never get it right."

That was exactly what I'd hoped. "Then I guess we'll just have to stay here until they do."

I'd have given up every possession I owned just to go back in time to that Olive Garden with her.

Even knowing how it would end.

Maybe especially knowing how it would end.

But I'd have given it all for one night where chicken parmesan was our only obstacle.

"Mr. Leblanc," Detective Rorke prompted, forcing me back to the present.

I closed my eyes and shook the memories off. "Right."

I motioned for Whit to evacuate the seat next to Elisabeth.

He moved swiftly, as though he knew that his future employment depended on it.

Elisabeth scooted her chair to the left, huffing as I followed.

"Okay," Rorke started, once again digging through his file. "We just have a few questions about Peach City Reproductive Center." He kept his head down but glanced up from his papers.

"Oh, okay," Elisabeth said, knotting her hands in her lap. "We, um, did in vitro fertilization there. It was—"

A stabbing pain hit me in the gut. "Is this about a bill?" I asked roughly, cutting her off. "I paid them years ago. If anything is still outstanding, I'll personally take care of it today."

Rorke faced me, but he watched Elisabeth from the corner of his eye. "I'm no collections agency, Mr. Leblanc. Ms. Keller, please continue."

Elisabeth's sad eyes lifted to his. "It was a good place is all I was going to say."

He jotted something on the paper in front of him. "And you were under the care of Dr. Fulmer during this time. Is that right?"

"Yes. He was amazing. Very understanding. Caring. Compassionate."

"And did this procedure with him produce a child? In vitro, I mean?"

Her green eyes fluttered closed as anguish carved her smooth, white skin. "Yes, but—"

I couldn't take any more. "What is this about?" I barked, desperate to regain the control I'd never had during the actual IVF process. Or in the years that followed, leading up to that very moment when I was being forced to watch Elisabeth relive the most painful experience of our lives.

"Just a few simple questions," Rorke said, all but dismissing me from the conversation.

I slammed my palm on the table and rose to my feet. "Discussing my son is not simple for anyone in this room but you."

"Roman!" Elisabeth scolded me for my outburst. But I'd have taken whatever heat she had to offer if it kept her from getting lost in the past.

I remained focused on Rorke. "Either tell me what this is about right fucking now or this interview is over."

"A son?" His eyes flashed wide, cutting to the mirrored wall before landing back on me.

"Tripp," Elisabeth breathed, pulling Rorke's eyes back to her. "He died within an hour of being born." She looked up and offered me a weak smile. "It's okay. I can do this."

Fan-fucking-tastic. She's reassuring me.

I bit the inside of my cheek and gripped the back of my neck.

"Son of a bitch," he mumbled under his breath. "And you didn't try again?"

"None of our embryos made it to freeze," she replied.

He once again cursed then steepled his fingers under his chin. "It's my understanding you can do another cycle for more embryos. How many cycles did you do with Dr. Fulmer?"

I sucked in a sharp breath, and Elisabeth shifted in her chair, crossing then uncrossing her legs.

"We didn't have the money for another fresh cycle," she admitted. "We had to clean out our savings and then borrow the rest from my parents to pay for the first one." She paused and then blurted, "Besides, Roman and I divorced six months after Tripp was born. There was no time. Even if there was money."

Wasn't that the damn truth.

Time was never on my side. Only months after our divorce, Rubicon had been created. If only she and I had stuck it out a few more weeks, I could have filled our house with a basketball team of children. She could have stayed pregnant for the rest of her natural life if that's what she'd wanted, and I would have happily lay on the floor, acting as a human jungle gym for each and every one of those kids, content for the rest of my life knowing I had given her that.

We could have been happy…again.

Fucking time.

"Was he buried?" Rorke asked, hope filling his eyes.

"Easy," I warned.

Elisabeth answered behind me. "Cremated."

"Dammit." Rorke closed his eyes, rubbing them with his thumb and his forefinger before opening them again. "I'm sorry, Ms. Keller, Mr. Leblanc. I'm sure this is a hard topic for both of you, so I'm going to be blunt here. We were unaware your son had passed away. We were hoping…" He stopped and trained his unfocused gaze on the door. "We were hoping to get a DNA sample from your son."

"Why?" Elisabeth and I asked in unison.

He leaned forward and lifted his pen off the table, tapping it to his chin as he answered. "We have reason to believe that Dr. Fulmer or one of his technicians accepted a bribe and possibly switched embryos in the lab. Your name was brought up during the questioning of a possible witness."

Elisabeth reacted immediately, reaching up and clamping my hand in hers, squeezing hard as she gasped.

Slowly sinking down to the chair, I rumbled, "I'm sorry. What did you just say?"

Rorke continued to explain. "I honestly can't get into specifics, as we are still looking into all avenues. But we were refused the warrants for DNA on the child in question due to a lack of evidence."

Elisabeth's hand flew up to cover her mouth. "The child?"

His shoulders rolled forward in defeat, but he nodded. "Yes, there is a possibility one of your embryos survived. But the supposed birth father has denied us all access. We were hoping to take the back door on this one, proving foul play based on your child's DNA. Then get the warrant once and for all."

I was vaguely aware of Whitman and Kaplin joining the conversation, tossing Rorke a million different questions laced with legal jargon, but my mind was spinning.

Bribes?

Embryos switched?

A child?

Our child?

It was a Thursday morning. I was supposed to be in a meeting with my marketing team, and instead, I was sitting in a police station, next to my ex-wife, finding out that we might have a child laughing, smiling, and breathing on Earth.

What the fucking hell was going on?

I finally swung my head to Elisabeth. Her face was pale, and tears streamed down her cheeks. Without thought or consideration, I snaked an arm out and looped it around her shoulders, pulling her into my side. She came all too willingly, crashing into my chest just before sobs overtook her.

CHAPTER SIX

ELISABETH

It was dark outside when I woke up on my couch. My heels were gone, but I was still in the same skirt and top I'd pulled on in a hurry that morning.

Police station.

"Oh God," I croaked.

I wasn't sure how I'd gotten home, but my feet must have moved at some point, even though my mind was still rooted in the middle of that police station.

Embryos switched.

"Oh God," I croaked.

Then I heard his voice in my kitchen.

"Cancel everything tomorrow and forward all of my calls to Glen. Yeah. No." Pause. Sigh. "I don't know when I'll be back. Let's just play this by ear."

Roman.

"Oh. God." I groaned, dragging my body up to the sitting position. My head objected, but I guessed that's what you got when you cried yourself dry of tears.

A child.

"Oh God," I breathed, dropping my face into my hands and settling my elbows on my knees.

"You're awake," Roman said, stating the obvious.

Out of the corner of my eye, I caught sight of his bare feet carrying him my way.

I closed my eyes and smarted, "You're in my house."

The couch sank beside me. Then I felt his hand on my back.

His strong, kind, gentle, *soothing* hand. *Damn it.* I screwed my eyes shut.

"How ya feeling?"

"Like I woke up in the Twilight Zone."

He chuckled. "Not far from the truth."

I scrubbed my face then did my best to smooth my sleep-mussed hair down. "Thanks for, um…bringing me home."

His hand moved up to the base of my neck, where it squeezed, massaging with his thumb before repeating the process on the other side. I lacked the energy to fight it and a pleasure-filled moan escaped my throat.

He chuckled again. "I ordered takeout."

His torturous hand continued kneading my neck, leaving me unable to argue. I hadn't eaten since earlier that morning. Food, even takeout, actually sounded amazing, and my stomach growled in agreement.

However, just as quickly, I lost my appetite.

"What the hell happened today?" I sighed listlessly.

His hand spasmed. Then it stilled for a brief second before continuing. "I don't know. But my people are looking into it."

Great.

Roman had *people* now.

And they were looking into the possibility that a child with my DNA was out there, sharing a world with *other people* I did not know.

Forget food. I needed to go back to sleep and hopefully wake up in a world that made sense.

"Oh God." I moaned, finally turning to face him. "Roman," I started, but the words froze on my tongue when I got my first real look at him—up close and personal.

He was still wearing his suit pants, but he'd shed the jacket and the button-down at some point since we'd arrived home. A simple, white undershirt clung to the hard ridges of his chest, the sleeves stretching mercifully around his thick biceps. I'd been wrong earlier that morning when I'd thought he was still just as gorgeous as he'd always been.

He was better.

And, a few years ago, I hadn't known that was possible.

He no longer sported the sexy stubble he'd insisted on growing after he'd gotten out of the military. Now, he was clean-shaven, not so much as a five-o'clock shadow marring his handsome face. His once barbershop-buzzed, dark-blond hair now bore the marks of a stylist—trimmed with precision on the sides, leaving the top longer and slightly unruly.

It all looked good on him.

Very good.

But he could look as mouthwateringly beautiful as he wanted to and it wouldn't change the man inside. And I couldn't risk getting tangled in the façade again.

Just because Roman was vowing his support right now, having his *people* look into things, didn't mean he'd stay to see this clusterfuck through. I'd watched him walk away too many times to willingly sign myself up for that again.

Besides, technically, he had no reason to be there.

And worse, no reason to stay.

During our long journey to have a child, we'd discovered that Roman produced very few sperm, most of which were abnormal. Doctors had been optimistic, saying that intrauterine insemination (IUI) would be our best bet. But, three miscarriages later, they changed their tune. The same day we were told that our last hope was in vitro fertilization (IVF), it was strongly suggested that we use a sperm donor. I did not deal with this news well.

First off, I knew we couldn't afford IVF. While we lived comfortably, we didn't have thirty to forty grand just lying around. We'd dropped most of our savings into our house when we'd gotten married and thought nothing of it. There had always been time to worry about savings later. We'd had each other. I'd like to say we were young and dumb. But what we really were was in love and eager to start a life together. A house seemed like the logical first step. We had no idea the financial burdens we'd be facing in the future. But, then again, making a baby with the man you loved was only supposed to cost a night of passion and an orgasm.

Secondly, the idea of having a child using donor sperm felt wrong on so many levels. I had a man I was madly in love with; I wanted *his* babies. Ones with his silver eyes and his mischievous smile. Little girls with his big heart and his thick lashes. I didn't just want kids; I wanted *his kids.*

I stormed out of the doctor's office that afternoon, pissed at a universe, who'd stolen the future we'd planned together, but I hadn't made it to my car before I was wrapped in his strong arms. He held my face in his neck while whispering promises that we'd find the money.

But money couldn't fix us.

A truth Roman had never fully grasped.

In the end, he was the one who insisted we move forward with a sperm donor. He smiled a gorgeous grin and told me, "Biology doesn't make families, Lissy. Love makes families."

Four months later, ten of my eggs were fertilized with a donor's sperm.

And, now, Roman was sitting on my couch, years after love had failed us, with only the biology of it all remaining.

I was the only thing tying him to this mess. I needed to cut him loose of his responsibilities once and for all.

Shifting away from him, I blurted, "I can handle this from here on out. No need for you to get involved."

His head snapped back. "Excuse me?"

"I just mean…. You know. You can go. I'll get back in touch with Detective Rorke and handle it from here. This isn't your problem."

His hand fell away from my back as he stared at me for several seconds. "This isn't my problem?"

"Well…no. This is *my* problem." I instinctively scooted over an inch, although I wasn't exactly sure why. Roman would never hurt me, but the pissed-off vibe radiating from his pores was suffocating.

He ominously swayed toward me. "*Your* problem?" His silver eyes darkened to a frightening shade of charcoal.

I leaned away. "I just meant—"

"Yeah, Lis. *Please*, tell me what you *just meant.*"

"I meant…" I carefully studied his face before I found the courage to say, "We aren't together anymore?" It came out as a question. "I just figured—"

I stopped talking when he moved closer, one hand on the back of the couch, the other on the arm, caging me into the corner.

"Say the words," he ordered on a pained whisper.

"I think you should leave."

"Not the words."

"Back up," I pleaded, but he got closer. Mere inches separated our bodies—less separated our mouths.

His breath breezed over my skin as he ground out, "*Still* not the words."

My pulse spiked at the same time my mouth dried.

He was too close.

Way, way, way too…

I closed my eyes.

He was wearing a different cologne, but the underlying smell of clean soap and shampoo was still my Roman, and the smell assaulted my olfactory senses at full force. But it was the subtle hit of beer on his breath that transported me back in time to a moment that seemed as though it had been nearly a million years ago, and it felt as though it had been even longer than that.

After numerous plates of chicken parmesan—all of which were wrong—Roman and I went out dancing at a hole-in-the-wall salsa bar downtown. Neither of us knew how to salsa, but we both made fools of ourselves trying to learn. I proved myself to be a quick study. Roman not so much, but he never quit. He also never took his eyes—or his hands—off me.

On the way home, we stopped at a food cart to pick up a two a.m. snack. Roman was almost as drunk as I was, and neither of us could stop laughing long enough to order.

"Two gyros. Extra Z. Add feta," he finally got out, blindly waving a twenty at the cashier. He pulled me into his arms and kissed the top of my hair.

"Oh my God, you ordered for me again." I feigned horror, playfully pushing him away.

He grinned with pride. "Sure did."

"And what if I don't like gyros?"

He swayed toward me, gliding his hand up the back of my neck and into my hair. "Everyone likes gyros."

"Not everyone," I laughed only to be silenced when he tilt-ed his head down and brushed his nose with mine.

He hadn't kissed me yet. I wasn't sure what the hold-up was, because God knows I'd given every signal I could think of—including a few I'd invented on the fly.

He dropped his forehead to mine and stayed close as I silently willed him closer.

When his mouth never made contact, I licked my lips and whispered, "I don't eat lamb."

His other arm hooked around my waist to bring our bod-ies flush. The intoxicating scent of clean sweat and beer invad-

ed my senses. I closed my eyes and breathed deeply, holding it in for as long as my lungs would allow, engraining it into my memory so I could never lose it—lose him.

As I exhaled, I felt his breath at my ear.

"It's a food cart, Lissy. I assure you these are beef."

It wasn't a sexy statement by anyone's standard, but it still made my knees weak.

Pressing my breasts against his chest, I raked my nails up his back. Then I whispered my own unsexy reply, "Oh. Okay, then. I like beef."

He stared at me for several beats, his eyes heating despite our ridiculous conversation.

My chest heaved impatiently.

Kiss me.

As though he'd heard my silent plea, his face split into a gorgeous grin.

A nanosecond later, in front of a food cart, while a dozen hungry drunks stumbled around us, Roman Leblanc changed my life.

But it wasn't with a kiss.

"Marry me," he breathed.

My eyes popped open.

"Say the words," he growled into my face.

"Roman, please." I pressed a hand to his chest and shimmied up the couch so he was no longer looming inches from my face—and my mouth. His eyes were still scary, but the way he watched me held more than just anger.

That might have been the most terrifying part of all.

"Look, I didn't mean that you *couldn't* be involved. I

only meant that you didn't *have* to be involved. You know…
because—"

"The kid wouldn't be mine," he finished for me.

Yes. Exactly that. "No. That's not it."

"Then. What. Is it?"

*Um…the kid's not yours, and you didn't exactly stick
around after the first one.*

"We aren't together anymore. I didn't figure you'd want
to get—"

"I swear to God, if you say involved, I'm going to lose
my mind."

I'd seen Roman lose his mind, and it was not pretty. I
valued my coffee table, so I bit my lip.

His jaw clenched as he sucked in a deep—and, I hoped,
calming—breath through his nose. "I'm well aware of the
fact that we aren't together *anymore*. I'm also aware that *we*
used a sperm donor. Not *you*. Not *me*. *We*. So whatever child
was or wasn't produced from that cycle of IVF is very much
ours." He arched an eyebrow, daring me to argue.

This was, in fact, the truth. But it wasn't as simple as he
made it out to be. There were a lot of factors in play, the biggest being my heart. I feared I wouldn't be able to handle it
if I gave him the only morsel of trust I had left only for him
to turn his back on me—again.

But he looked really pissed, so I didn't dare fill him in
on that.

Instead, I kept my mouth shut and nodded in agreement. I could write him a letter informing him of such after
I'd moved to an undisclosed location where he couldn't find
me and pin me to a couch.

"That means I'm *involved* in this one hundred percent," he stated.

I nodded again, fighting the urge to amend with, *Until you get too busy at work to worry about anything else—including, but not limited to, me.*

"So I'll repeat. My people are looking into it"—he paused and studied my eyes—"for *us*."

I had a million things to say to the man who had broken my heart and was now claiming he wanted to be *involved*. None of them were going to get him off me so I could think clearly though. So I went with, "What's for dinner?"

He stared for a moment longer, and then a huge grin broke across his face. "Gyros."

CHAPTER SEVEN

ROMAN

"**A**re you insane!" she laughed.

There was a strong possibility that I was drunk, but I wasn't insane.

I also wasn't kidding.

I'd known Elisabeth for a matter of hours, and I knew with an absolute certainty that I wanted to spend the rest of my life with her.

Sure, it was crazy and impulsive, but it was so fucking right.

So I repeated, "Marry me."

"I don't even know you. We've had one date, and you fed me the wrong chicken parmesan. That doesn't exactly scream husband material." She shot me a gleaming, white smile.

"It was only wrong because you gave up. It's not my fault you called it quits after plate number seven. I was committed to the cause."

66

"Your cause was wasting seven plates of chicken parmesan. You know there are starving kids in Africa, right?" She giggled and buried her face in my neck.

"Is that a yes?" I asked, sifting my fingers through the back of her hair.

Her head jerked up, those deep-green eyes smiling nearly as much as her lips. "Um, no. It's a definite no. However, despite the fact that I now think you have mental issues, I will agree to a second date."

I teasingly squinted at her, and she bit her lips to stifle a laugh.

"Fine, but you should probably head home and pack your belongings, because that date starts now and it's going to be so long it lasts a lifetime."

She barked a laugh. "So, like, say…a marriage?"

"Yes. Exactly like a marriage. Phew. I'm so glad we agree."

She shook her head and whispered, "Insane."

I trailed my lips up her neck to her ear and whispered, "Say yes."

"No."

I grazed my teeth over her earlobe. "Say yes."

"No," she gasped, throwing her head back. The ends of her long hair tickling my hand at her back.

Unable to stop myself, I placed a kiss on the soft flesh at the base of her neck. As chills spread across her skin, I murmured, "You know you feel it, too."

Fisting the back of my shirt, she moaned. "I'd like to feel more. Let's go back to my place."

I could give her more.

But I was taking forever.

I glided my hand from her hair to cup her jaw and drank her in. She wasn't particularly tall, even in heels, so at six two, I had her by several inches, but the way her body fit against mine was nothing short of perfection. Her makeup had started to melt, and her lipstick had been left on the lips of the wineglasses at the bar. But she was still stunning. I couldn't explain why I'd fallen head over heels for that woman as quickly as I had, but I knew I was never letting her go. Whether it took a month, a year, or a decade, I was going to make her say yes.

Sweeping my lips across hers, I murmured, "Fine. I'm not above coercing you into marriage with my sexual prowess."

She laughed so loud that I would have been offended—if I hadn't already been in love with her.

"Where'd you get beer?" Elisabeth asked as she scrambled from the couch.

"Seth," I replied, hanging my head and rubbing my eyes.

Jesus, I'd wanted to kiss her. She was being a bitch, spouting shit she didn't mean just because she was too scared to let me in.

But, even through it, those plump lips were calling to me.

I'd never been able to resist that woman. Despite that we'd fallen apart, it hadn't changed. The hum for her was still in my veins. It never went away, but for two years, it had been dormant. I'd packed it down so tightly that I'd hoped it had died. But, with one look, my body began thrumming like a live wire.

"Seth?" she asked as she bent over to straighten her tight, black pencil skirt.

It was a rare occasion to catch Elisabeth in something other than a perfectly pressed skirt and a pair of heels. But she'd been sleeping all day. It was wrinkled all to hell and back. The only thing her efforts succeeded in was drawing my attention down to her legs.

Legs that had spent many nights wrapped around my hips as she came while crying my name.

Shit. I should go.

But, after the way she'd latched on to me that morning, I wasn't going anywhere.

"My assistant," I answered. "I had him pick you up a bottle of wine, too."

She blinked. "You have an assistant? Who delivers you beer? And your ex-wife wine?"

"No, I have an assistant who does whatever the fuck I need him to do. And, luckily for us, beer and wine happen to fall into the whatever-the-fuck-I-need-him-to-do category tonight." She fought back a smile as I finished, "So do gyros."

"Damn. I need to get one of those," she mumbled to herself.

I smirked. "Cash my checks and you could afford one."

It was a dick move, bringing up the money right then. But, despite her expert hand in decorating, that little starter house we'd bought with rose-colored glasses now needed a shit-ton of work.

Her back shot ramrod straight, fury crinkling the corners of her eyes as she snarled, "I'm *not* cashing your checks."

I shrugged. "Guess you'll have to figure out how to get your own wine and dinner after tonight."

"I think I can manage," she fired back.

"Suit yourself." I pushed off the couch and meandered to the kitchen.

I went to the fridge and leaned in, searching for anything I could snack on. With the exception of at least a dozen Tupperware containers, she didn't have much in the way of a quick bite.

Snagging a handful of grapes from the drawer, I made a mental note to send Seth to the grocery store after he'd delivered dinner.

Popping the grapes in my mouth one by one, I felt her watching me in what could only be defined as silent awe. I decided my best move would be to ignore it. "You know, I should have invented Tupperware. You alone could keep me in business," I told her, retrieving a beer and then shutting the door.

She scoffed then muttered, "At least then I would have benefitted from you abandoning our marriage."

Lava fresh off the volcanoes in Hell boiled in my veins.

I cocked my head to the side and questioned, "I'm sorry. Come again?"

"You should go," she snapped.

Think a-fucking-gain.

"Nah, I'm good. Got any movies?"

I tipped the bottle to my lips, doing my best to calm the storm brewing within me, all while still fighting the desire to take her to the floor, plant myself between her legs, and remind her how that fucking attitude affected me.

Clearly, she had forgotten.

My cock had not.

"Roman, it's been a crazy day. Please don't do this tonight."

"Do what?" I asked, leaning back against the huge, granite island.

She threw her hands out to the sides in frustration. "What you always do."

"What do I always do, *Lissy*?"

"This!" she yelled.

I frowned and took another pull from my beer. "Haven't been in our kitchen, drinking beer, in a long time. I hardly think it's fair to say I *always* do it."

Her eyes nearly bulged from her head. "*My* kitchen, Roman. This is *my* kitchen. Not ours. And you know good and damn well that is *not* what I'm talking about."

My lips twitched as I pointed the neck of my bottle at her. "No. What I know good and damn well is that I have *no* idea what the fuck you are talking about. Or why you're slinging unnecessary and, might I add, undeserved attitude at me like a short-order cook at the bitch house."

"He did not say that to me," she whispered to herself.

When I lifted a shoulder in a half shrug, she swung a pointed finger toward the door and yelled, "Get out!"

I grinned, crossing my legs at the ankle. "You always were cranky when you were hungry."

And that was the exact moment her head exploded.

"We are done here!" she declared, aiming her finger back at me. "Not another word more. I'll hire an attorney tomorrow, and he'll be in touch with yours regarding whatever our next step is with the cops. Hopefully, we can file something with the courts and get them to issue a DNA test or…whatever. But, in the meantime, you are *not* standing here in *my* kitchen, drinking *my* beer." She paused and sucked in a deep breath. "Yes! *My* beer, I don't give a shit if your fancy-ass assistant did deliver it. It's in m*y* fridge. In *my* house. It's *my* beer!"

I moved. And I did it so fast that she didn't have a chance to react before she was up against my chest. "I don't give a damn whose beer it is."

"Let go of me." She fought in my grasp.

"Not until you listen. While you were busy crying into *my* chest. And holding *my* shoulders like you couldn't get close enough. Then falling asleep in *my* arms like it was the only place you ever fucking belonged." I gripped the back of her hair and tipped her head back, leaning in close as I added, "Which it fucking *is*."

The fight left her. Her body sagging in my arms, even as her eyes flashed wide.

Trailing my thumb back and forth over her cheek, I finished with, "I got some information from the cops. I'm not here to fight with you, so calm down, share a meal and a much-needed glass of wine with me, and let me fill you in."

"Roman," she exhaled, her eyes flooding with tears.

I wasn't sure what part of that had softened her—or I would have repeated it.

Again.

And again.

And maybe a hundred times after that.

Because, with just the sound of my name, she gave me my innocent angel back.

And it was that moment when I realized it had been a

God's-honest miracle I'd been able to breathe a single breath in the two years I'd lived without her.

It was also then that I decided those days were done.

"You know we could be civil to each other." I smiled. It was only a half lie. Because there was nothing *civil* about the things I wanted to do to her.

She would, however, enjoy them all.

"Fine. Fill me in. Eat your gyro, but then you have to leave. I seriously can't do this with you tonight."

My hand flexed on her back as I dropped my lips to her ear and murmured, "No. Then I'm sleeping on your couch."

"Roman!" she objected just as there was a knock at the door.

I kissed the top of her head and released her. "Dinner's here. Get out the plates."

She complained behind me as I sauntered to the front door before pulling it wide.

Only it wasn't Seth on the other side.

CHAPTER EIGHT

CLARE

Walter had been gone when I'd woken up.

Like I did every time he walked out our front door, I'd prayed that he wouldn't come home. Accidents happened. And, in his line of work, people died every day.

But I was never that lucky.

Walter Noir would crawl a million miles through broken glass, bleeding and dying, just to make sure he took me to Hell with him.

I'd put on my workout clothes and packed my bag first thing that morning, strategically placing it on the table closest to the door, along with my water bottle and my car keys. Then I'd gone about my day, playing with my daughter while simultaneously listening for his car to pull through the iron gates of my prison.

Around five, I heard the rumble of his BMW, so I rushed

to the bag, threw it over my shoulder, grabbed Tessa off the floor, and darted out the door.

He wasn't happy that I was leaving just as he was getting home, but it wasn't as if I'd planned it that way. Or so I swore as he kissed me goodbye before I made my getaway to the gym.

Tessa was tired, so was I, but I had two hours of quasi-freedom ahead of me.

Two hours he wouldn't be around Tessa, and by the time we got home, I could feed her dinner, give her a bath, and put her straight to bed. Minimal contact was the best I could hope for when it came to Walt.

A rush of relief washed over me as I pulled into a parking spot at the gym. I slowly climbed from the car, my ribs only protesting mildly, a huge step up from the day before. My injuries were still visible, but they were thankfully starting to heal. The real agony was in the memories—and my reality.

I was unbuckling Tessa from her car seat when I heard a man call my name. I turned and found two uniformed police officers closing in on me. Panic slammed into me like a runaway truck.

In my life, the police were the only entity more frightening than Walt.

Walt could kill me, but cops could take my life by locking me away, leaving Tessa alone in the care of a monster.

I spun away with shaking hands, scrambling to get Tessa out of her seat.

"Mrs. Noir," one of them called as I collected her bag off the floor and sped toward the gym door. "Mrs. Noir," he repeated more firmly before a hand on my bicep suddenly halted me. "Mrs. Noir, a word?"

Doing my best to keep the tremor out of my voice, I replied, "I'm sorry. I don't have time." I pulled my arm from his grasp and started away.

I came to a sharp stop when the young officer smiled and reached out his hand as though he were about to touch her.

"This must be Tessa."

My soul caught fire.

The panic was gone in a blink, and a feral blaze overwhelmed me. Instinctively shifting her to my other hip, I twisted so my body was between her and the officer, blocking any possible contact.

"Don't you dare touch her," I spat.

"Jesus, Marco. Don't touch the baby," a different man scolded from behind him.

I glanced up to see an older man prowling up behind the uniforms. Salt-and-pepper hair. Potbelly. Shiny, gold badge showing from underneath his sports coat.

Fuck.

He looked professional.

Flashing my eyes back to Marco, I stumbled back a step as the men closed in around me.

"Calm down, Clare," the older guy urged while I backed away, feeling like a caged animal. "We're not here to cause any trouble," he assured.

"Then back up," I returned.

He lifted a hand and both officers came to a sudden halt. I was able to put a few more feet between us before he spoke again.

"Better?"

"I'd be better if you left."

He pointed toward the now scabbed-over cut over my eye and said, "I don't doubt that's the truth, but we need to have a word. You're a hard woman to track down."

That's because I wasn't allowed to leave our house and it would have to be swallowed by a sinkhole in order for Walt to allow emergency personnel through the front gate.

"Not hard enough, apparently," I shot back.

He grinned and then gave a chin lift. "Boys, give us a minute."

They didn't delay in following his order.

I was far from in the clear, but I instantly felt better now that I wasn't boxed in anymore.

"Now, is *that* better?" he asked.

I didn't answer his question, but with no one at my back, I once again started toward the door.

"Mrs. Noir, we need to talk."

I didn't. I needed to get inside.

"I'm sorry. If you have something to discuss, please contact my attorney and make an appointment," I called, tucking Tessa's face into my neck.

She was oblivious to what was happening, more content to play with the small, gold chain at my neck—another of Walt's "gifts"—but I still hated that she was involved at all.

"Clare, my name is Charles Rorke. I'm a detective with the APD, and I've spoken with your husband's attorney more than I have my own wife this week. Your husband has refused to speak to us, so I'm here, attempting to talk to *you*."

"I have nothing to say." I turned to walk away.

"Not even about the fact that Tessa might not be biologically yours?" he told my back.

Cops hated me. Well, actually, they hated Walt. And then me by association. But never in my life had anyone been crueler—and that was saying a lot, considering I was married to a man who beat me on a near daily basis.

But that, whatever angle he was going for, was scraping the bottom of the barrel.

"You son of a bitch," I breathed, turning to face him. A surge of adrenaline made me strong—physically and emotionally. Taking a step toward him, I squared my shoulders. "You show up here to ask me a few questions while spouting shit like that?"

"I wish it were shit, Clare. But we're investigating the possibility of criminal activity involving Peach City Reproductive Center."

"Oh, screw you." I started to walk away when the Earth suddenly crumbled under my feet.

"We have reason to believe that Walter Noir was involved in a situation that led to embryos purposely being switched in the lab!" he shouted at my back.

I froze, my legs nearly buckling.

A meteor could have fallen from the sky and I couldn't have moved.

"Walter Noir was involved in a situation."

Now, *that* I could believe. Walter Noir was involved in *every situation,* especially those that would hurt *me.* And this would rip the heart straight from my chest.

My nose began to sting as I desperately fought an onslaught of tears back.

I dropped the gym bag from my arm and shifted Tessa to my other hip. Then, cupping my hand at the side of her head, I covered her ears as though it could stop me from hearing it all.

"What?" I croaked.

His body slacked, and his voice softened. "I see he hasn't mentioned our conversations to you."

"What?" I repeated, tears finally breaching my lids.

"We need a DNA sample from Tessa, Clare. That is the only way we can prove this once and for all." He took a step toward me before reaching out to give my shoulder a reassuring squeeze.

I didn't back away. That would have required the use of my legs, and it was a miracle they were still holding me upright.

"What?" I repeated once again, like a skipping CD unable to move forward.

I was dazed, my mind frantically trying to keep up, when I saw the giant approach out of the corner of my eye.

"Back the fuck up," he ordered.

I lifted my eyes and found Brock, one of Walt's trusty henchmen, stepping in front of me. He must have arrived for "Clare duty" just in time.

"Walt won't consent to the DNA, Clare," the detective spoke around him. "We need this from you."

"Don't fucking talk to her." Brock moved closer to Rorke.

The uniformed officers quickly reappeared.

"Not another move!" Marco shouted.

I couldn't keep up. Someone had pressed fast forward while my mind was still stuck in slow motion.

"Don't do it. Don't you fucking do it!" Marco shouted while Brock issued his own angry orders at the officers.

"Put your fucking hands up!" was the last thing I heard before I felt an arm wrap around my stomach and begin to drag me backward.

"Clare!" Rorke called just as I heard, "Come with me, Clare," whispered in my ear.

Luke.

And, finally, I crumbled.

My breath rushed from my mouth on a wail as I allowed him to pull Tessa from my arms.

"Shit," he cursed, supporting the majority of my weight on one side, Tessa on his other as he guided us into the gym and straight to his office.

Safety.

He planted me in a chair then settled Tessa in my lap long enough to unroll a yoga mat and dig a notebook and a bunch of highlighters out for her to draw with.

I was so numb that I couldn't even argue with him that I was okay.

There was no brave face anymore.

Tessa might not be your biological child, rang in my ears.

Once he had her settled, he crouched in front of me and finally asked, "What the hell is going on?"

The right answer was, *Nothing.*

The right thing to do was put a smile on, forget everything that had happened out in the parking lot, and go about the day like I hadn't just been served the most severe beating of my life.

It was the safest thing for everyone involved.

But, for reasons lost on even myself, I threw my arms around his neck and spilled it all.

Luke didn't hug me back. Instead, he kept both hands anchored to the arms of my chair as he balanced in front of me. I didn't need the physical contact; I just needed someone to listen.

I was going to get him killed, but the words wouldn't stop flowing from my mouth.

I told him about the drug trafficking.

Walt's ties to organized crime.

The murders he'd made me clean up.

The money laundering.

The beatings.

The blood.

The fear.

The prison he kept me in.

And finally.

Tessa.

Why, after all the years of having kept it locked away, I chose to unload it all on a personal trainer, I'd never understand. But finding out that my only reason to wake up the next morning might not even be mine was the final straw.

After I'd told him about what had gone down in the parking lot, I fell silent.

The weight of the world still heavily rested on my shoulders, but the load somehow felt lighter. And, for the briefest of seconds, I took a deep breath for the first time since Walter Noir had walked into my life.

Luke didn't immediately respond, and I couldn't blame him.

Finding out the scum of the Earth was doing push-ups right under your nose had to be a hard pill to swallow.

After peeling my arms from around his neck, he placed them in my lap and rocked back on his heels. His blue eyes flashed to Tessa then back to me, his face steeled with confidence as he asked, "How can I help?"

Christ, he was a good guy.

I laughed through my tears. "You can't. No one can."

He opened his mouth to reply when a booming, "Where the fuck is my wife!" came from outside the door.

I jumped, and Tessa started crying. After shooting to my feet, I plucked her off the floor and prepared for the worst.

It was Walt.

The worst was all I ever got.

CHAPTER NINE

ELISABETH

"No," Roman growled, slamming the door less than a second after he'd opened it.

"What the—" Kristen cried from the other side.

He glared at me over his shoulder, frustration floating in the air around him.

I couldn't fight my smile back.

"Elisabeth!" she yelled, shaking the door handle in an attempt to get in.

I sauntered past Roman, using my shoulder to nudge him out of the way, and yanked the door open.

As if his sister were an axe murder, he stepped close to my back, protectively looping an arm around my waist.

It was then that I worried Roman could possibly be an axe murder, because if he thought he was claiming me like that after having pinned me to the couch and proclaimed he was sleeping there that night, he had serious mental concerns that needed to be addressed ASAP.

And what better way than with his sister at my side for his intervention.

Kristen's mouth gaped as her eyes drifted down to his arm.

I grabbed his wrist and roughly removed it. "Hey," I said casually.

"Dear God, did I hit a time loop?" Her gaze went to her brother. "Quick! What year is it?"

"Better question is what the hell are you doing here?" he sniped back.

She narrowed her eyes. "No. I believe the best question is how in the hell you were able to cross this threshold without Liz lighting you on fire." Her gaze drifted back to me, her eyebrow arching in accusation. "I thought that was the plan if he showed up. Shit, Liz. Mom even bought the lighter fluid."

I giggled because she was *not* kidding. Cathy Leblanc loved her son, and when shit had gone down with Roman and me, she'd made it clear she would not be taking sides between her "children." But, the day after Roman exchanged our entire life for fifty percent of his precious company, she showed up at my door with a bottle of wine and a can of lighter fluid. About three weeks later, she must have had a change of heart, because she showed up with a bottle of wine and a fire extinguisher. "*Just in case*," were her words.

Kristen impatiently cocked her head to the side, insisting on a verbal answer.

"Some things...well, happened today," I stammered out.

Kristen was family, but I was in no rush to tell people about what had happened at the police station. We didn't know for certain if there was anything to tell. It could have been some huge mix-up nothing ever came of.

Or it could have been some huge mix-up where Roman and I had another child—one who'd lived longer than twelve minutes.

My eyes closed painfully. "Oh God," I whispered.

Roman's arm once again folded around my waist, and this time, I didn't fight. I swayed back against his chest.

"Uh, are y'all back together?" Kristen asked.

My eyes popped open as I declared, "No."

However, just as quickly, I heard Roman say, "Maybe."

I jerked from his hold on me and glanced over my shoulder. "What? No!" I insisted.

He shot me an arrogant grin then repeated, "Maybe."

"Roman!" I yelled, all but stomping my foot.

He ignored me completely and turned his attention back to his sister. "What are you doing here?"

She was watching us with a wide smile that said she really liked the idea of Roman's *maybe*.

Traitor!

Lifting a paper bag in the air, she replied to him, "Convincing her."

"Ah!" he said in understanding.

I, however, was clueless. "Convincing me of what?"

They both ignored me.

"You gonna let me in or not?" she asked.

This time, our responses were reversed.

Roman quickly snapped, "No."

85

While I replied, "Maybe."

Her eyebrows shot up as she suppressed a laugh. "Maybe?"

"Depends. What are you trying to convince me of?"

She shrugged. "Nothing now. Seems my little brother is going to be doing his own version of convincing."

Roman chuckled.

I swung a glare between the two of them that would have frozen normal people, but unfortunately, there was nothing normal about either one of them.

"No one is doing any convincing," I declared.

"Okay," they replied in unison.

That was a bad sign. A really fucking bad sign. It meant they were going to be secretly convincing, which was eleventy billion times worse than normal convincing, and it also guaranteed that I would ultimately *be* convinced, because I knew they wouldn't stop until I was. It was the Leblanc way.

I cursed under my breath, which earned me a mouth-watering smirk from Roman and a sugary-sweet smile from Kristen.

I groaned and moved from the doorway to allow her entry.

She didn't hesitate in accepting the invitation. "I brought sushi and wine."

"Roman's *assistant* is delivering gyros," I smarted.

She stopped midway to the kitchen, cutting her gaze to her brother, and hissed, "Seth?"

Roman rolled his eyes before tagging the bag from her hand, carrying it to the counter, and unceremoniously plopping it down. "I'm not firing the guy."

"You have *got* to be kidding!" she returned, charging after him.

"Wait." I jogged to keep up. "This is *Seth* Seth? The asshole Seth who never called back, Seth? Seth the nice cock, all night long, Seth?"

"Jesus, fuck. Seriously?" Roman grumbled. "I don't need to know that shit."

"I thought we discussed this!" she told his back.

He got busy pulling the sushi from the bag. "You talked. I listened. But what I did not do is agree to fire a man because things did not work out with my sister. This being after I told my sister not to pursue something with one of my employees."

Lasers shot from Kristen's eyes, but Roman's aura seemed impenetrable.

He lifted a pair of chopsticks in the air and asked, "Did you get extra wasabi?"

I swiftly stepped between the two of them, fearing a brawl in the middle of my kitchen. That brawl being a verbal one but no less messy.

"Okay, okay. Let's chill out."

"Where's the lighter fluid?" Kristen questioned, glowering at her brother as he shoved a piece of sashimi in his mouth, completely unaffected.

A laugh sprang from my throat, causing all eyes to swing my way.

"I'm sorry," I told Kristen. "It's just…" *I miss this.* I continued to laugh and waved the rest of my statement off.

I glanced back at Roman and found him leaning against the counter, his weight resting on his hip, his legs crossed at the ankle, a smile showing on his chewing mouth.

Gorgeous.

And comfortable.

And so fucking right.

Oh God.

I kept laughing because it felt amazing for the first time in as long as I could remember.

Do not get used to this.

"Wine?" I asked through a giggle just as another knock came.

Kristen was immediately off and stomping to the door.

I started to go after her, fearing a brawl of a different nature, when Roman caught my bicep.

"Don't," he ordered, sliding an arm around my waist.

Chills swirled down my spine as he bent to whisper in my ear.

"Just because I'm not firing Seth doesn't mean he's not an asshole. He deserves whatever fury she's about to rain down upon him." His lips swept my neck, and regardless of what my mind was screaming, my body shifted into his side and my hand moved to the firm ridges of his stomach.

It was as though the connection completed a full circuit, because the hairs on the back of my neck prickled and a heat only Roman Leblanc could give me pooled between my legs.

One simple touch and I was ready.

I'd always been that way with him though.

After we ate our "beef" gyros, we strolled to my apartment, talking, laughing, and making out in every alley we stumbled across. By the time we'd gotten to my door, his hand was down the front of my shirt and I was exploring the hard planes of his chest.

My neighbors, should they have been up at three a.m., were going to get a show. But I couldn't have cared less. Roman had that way about him. He made me forget the world around me. He was enough. And, together, we were everything. I knew that even though I'd only had him in my life for one day.

I'd laughed at his proposal. But maybe I was the crazy one for not saying yes immediately. It was wrong though; people didn't get engaged on their first date.

If only I could explain why I so badly wanted to say yes.

"Roman," I breathed, swinging my door open as he swept my panties to the side, one finger sliding inside me.

"Fuck. Me," he murmured before laving his tongue up my neck. His mouth trailed kisses up to my ear as his husky voice rumbled. "So fucking ready for me."

I was.

So fucking ready for all of him.

"Roman," I moaned, tipping my head to the side to allow him better access.

His finger hooked inside me, sending a rush of ecstasy through me.

"More," I pleaded, my head falling back as I struggled to stay on my feet.

His strong arm looped around my hips, keeping me upright. He removed his fingers and lifted me off my feet so I dangled inches off the ground as he sidestepped us into my apartment.

"Get the door, baby," he ordered.

Baby.

I'd have done anything he wanted if it was proceeded with the smooth sound of baby falling from his lips.

With a kick, I slammed the door shut.

Suddenly, we were alone, and as his mouth sealed over mine, our tongues gloriously gliding together, I wasn't sure I ever wanted to open the door again.

His frenzied hands gentled long enough to lower me to the floor. My couch was mere feet away, but we hadn't had the time nor the desire to make it that far.

His hard body covered mine, his hips falling between my open legs.

Then my shirt was off in a matter of seconds, and my skirt quickly followed.

"Fuck, Lis," he grunted, sliding down my body. His finger curled in the top of my bra, tugging it down before taking my nipple between his lips. His warm tongue swirled and his teeth nipped, shooting sparks that rivaled any orgasm I'd ever had straight to my clit.

"Roman," I moaned, arching my back and pressing more of my breast into his mouth.

He growled, the vibrations coaxing me closer to the edge. His hair was too short to thread my fingers through, so I palmed the back of his head, holding him as though he were attempting to get away. He absolutely wasn't.

I lifted my hips when I felt the tips of his fingers start their descent down my stomach.

Our groans harmonized as he dipped his fingers between my legs and pressed in just enough to taunt me.

"Please," I begged.

His head popped up to catch my gaze. "Given any more thought to that proposal?" he asked with a smirk that was all Roman Leblanc.

And, therefore, I didn't just see it—I felt it. Deep inside, where no other man had ever been.

"This is crazy," I told him, spreading my legs wide.

"I know," he whispered, holding my gaze as he slid two fingers inside me.

I writhed, driving myself down, unable to get close enough.

I needed more. Not the kind of more his body could offer.

I wanted the kind of more that spoke to my soul that only Roman had to offer.

His hand worked me, pumping in and out, taking me closer and closer to the edge.

"Roman, I—"

"Shh... It's okay, baby. Offer's on the table. Whenever you're ready, I'll be here. All you have to do is say yes." He dropped his thumb to my clit and skillfully circled.

As an orgasm so strong that I feared I'd never be able to recover tore through me, I realized I was absolutely ready for anything and everything as long as it was with him.

"Mmm," Roman purred into the top of my hair, snapping me out of my thoughts. I was plastered against his side, my hand fisting the front of his shirt, my cheeks heated, and my legs nearly shaking. Cupping my chin, he tipped my head back so he could meet my gaze. "What are you thinking about, babe?"

Nope. No way was I answering that question.

Luckily, I didn't have to because, just as Kristen pulled open the door, ready to give Seth the tongue-lashing of his life, the air went static.

"Oh shit," Kristen mumbled, glancing back at me, her eyes wide with apology.

His gaze found mine over the top of Kristen's head. It dropped to my hand on Roman's stomach as he said, "Liz?"

CHAPTER TEN

ROMAN

"**J**on. Hey!" she said in surprise, immediately evacuating her position at my side and hurrying toward the door. "Wh-what are you doing here?"

The man's eyes focused on me as he absently answered, "You didn't show up at the Victorian. Been calling for the last hour. I got worried."

I trailed after her, doing my best not to show the rage boiling in my veins or the sour churning in my gut.

For the love of all that's holy, don't let this be her boyfriend.

She stepped in front of Kristen, forcing her to move from the doorway. "Shit. I'm sorry. Today's been crazy."

Jon's gaze flashed to mine as he shifted awkwardly in the doorway. "I can see."

It hadn't exactly been said in an asshole tone, but that was up for interpretation. However, just the fact that he was standing in Elisabeth's doorway had my interpretation skewed—and not in his favor.

Shoving my hand over her shoulder to offer a shake, I smiled something that I hoped read: *Hi, how ya doing?* Meanwhile, my eyes read: *If you've ever touched her, that shit is officially over.* But it was my mouth that said, "I don't believe we've met. I'm Roman Leblanc, Elisabeth's husband."

Her body went solid before she corrected, "Ex! Ex-husband."

I shrugged and kept my eyes on *Jon* as I stated, "That's debatable."

"It's not debatable!" she yelled over her shoulder at me. Then she looked back at the asshole and said, "He's my *ex-husband.*"

"We're still figuring that part out," I amended.

Jon's eyes bounced between us as he silently took us in. By the frustration and disappointment coloring his face, he was coming to the correct conclusion.

Or at least correct as far as I was concerned.

Elisabeth was on a slightly different page.

"We're not figuring anything out!" she exclaimed, shoving my unshaken hand back over her shoulder. "Come on, Jon. Let's talk on the porch."

I should have let her go. I had no reason to be jealous. The connection Elisabeth and I shared was undeniable, no matter how much she tried to pretend she hated me. Hell, she had reason to hate me, but she'd spent the day in my arms, reminding me that I'd been living half of a life for the last two years. And, moments before this guy had arrived, her face had been red, her hand had been clutching my shirt, and a soft moan had escaped her throat. There was no fucking way I was losing that.

She might have been confused about who she belonged to.

But Jon would not walk out of that house without being fully informed.

Stepping in front of her, I slid a hand up her neck and into her hair, gently fisting until it forced her head back. Her breath caught as I leaned into her face, and I took great pleasure in the goose bumps that pebbled her smooth skin.

Brushing my nose with hers, I whispered, "Hurry up, baby. Sushi's waiting."

She stared, her lips parting as I licked my own. She was in my trance. I recognized it because I'd been lost in hers for nearly a decade.

Ever so slightly, she tipped her chin up, offering me the lips I was starved for. I could have taken her right there in front of Kristen, Jon, and the entire fucking city of Atlanta and she would have *come* willingly.

"Always so fucking ready for me," I murmured.

I wanted to kiss her—and never stop.

Unless it was to move my mouth between her legs.

At the thought, a low sound rumbled in my throat, and she suddenly came alert.

She blinked once, twice, and then I lost her.

Her hand went to my shoulder, shoving roughly as she seethed, "Let me go."

Tightening my fist in her hair, I whispered, "Never," before releasing her. Smiling at the man fuming in the doorway, I called out, "Nice to meet you, Jon," as I casually turned and walked back to the kitchen.

When I heard the front door slam behind me, my shoulders fell and I closed my eyes. Pinching the bridge of my nose, I propped myself up on a white-knuckled fist on the island.

"Wow," Kristen breathed behind me. "That was…"

Fuck. Time to be bitched at.

I lifted a hand to silence her. "I don't want to hear it. I need a fucking drink, not a lecture."

Her open hand landed hard on my shoulder, and my eyes popped open.

"Holy shit! That was incredible." She laughed.

A shy smile tipped one side of my lips. I asked nervously, "Yeah? You think?"

"Roman! She hated you yesterday, and I swear to God she just came from that whole hand-in-the-hair bit." She wrapped both hands in the front of my shirt and shook me. "Oh my God! You're gonna get Elisabeth back!"

I barked a laugh of relief. "I'm sure as hell gonna try," I told her.

She squealed, jumping into my arms like we were kids again.

Movement outside the front window caught my attention. Elisabeth's feet swayed back and forth in the porch swing, Jon's right beside her, which reminded me that we had a long way to go before we could celebrate anything.

"Okay, stop." I used her shoulders to shift her off me. "I need you to fill me in on everything about his guy so I know what I'm up against."

"Who? Jon?"

"No, the other man sitting on a swing I hung in a house that I bought and doing it all while sitting next to *my* wife."

She attempted a glare, but her smile was too wide to give it any heat.

She headed toward the fridge and pulled two beers out, passing me one before starting. "Okay, so Jon…"

⸙

Two beers later, I was sitting on the corner of the island when Elisabeth came back inside carrying a plastic bag filled with to-go boxes.

She lifted them in the air, saying, "I decided to save Seth from certain death."

"That son of a bitch," Kristen cursed.

I chuckled, tipping the beer to my lips and hopping down to meet her.

She passed the bags off to me, but her eyes never met mine as she headed straight for the glass of wine I had waiting for her on the counter.

"Soooo, how's Jon?" Kristen asked.

"He's good," she replied between gulps of her Chardonnay, not looking at either of us.

"Everything okay?" Kristen pushed.

"Yep," Elisabeth answered curtly, going to work on removing the boxes from the bags I'd set on the counter. She robotically opened each before closing it and sliding it down the counter to make room for the next. Once they were all laid out, she opened the cabinet above her and retrieved two plates.

97

Two.

Not three.

Two.

I felt Kristen's gaze cut to me, but I was studiously watching Elisabeth's back as she removed gyros from their boxes and delicately placed them on the blue, floral plates we'd received as a wedding gift. After she got every fry in place, she set one beside Kristen and the other beside me. Then she finally lifted her gaze.

I flinched when I got a look at the pain etched into her face. It was a look I knew well—*defeat*.

Shit. Maybe Kristen was wrong and this Jon guy actually means something to Elisabeth.

"Lissy," I breathed, reaching out to her.

She took a step away and aimed her eyes at the floor. "Y'all go ahead and eat. Just let yourself out whenever you're done. I'm gonna call it a night."

"Elisabeth," Kristen called, but she only lifted a hand in a wave and rushed from the room.

I moved to follow her but stopped at the foot of the stairs as she disappeared up to the top.

"What the hell was that?" Kristen asked after we'd both heard the bedroom door quietly close.

I raked a hand through the top of my hair. "No clue. You're sure about this Jon guy?"

"Positive. No way that's about him." Kristen appeared at my side, offering one of the plates of food my way. "Here. Go after her. I'll let the dog in and lock up."

I nodded, but my feet remained stuck. That expression on Elisabeth's face had been like a knife from the past, gutting me all over again. She had worn that look of heart-breaking despondency every time I'd seen her after Tripp died. Back then, I didn't know how to fix it. I thought that, if I could give her another baby, maybe, just maybe, I could make it all go away and bring the vibrant woman who'd stolen my heart back.

I physically couldn't do it. Fertility just wasn't on my side.

And it killed me that I wasn't financially able to do it either. I was a soldier who had gotten out of the military with hopes and dreams of starting my own consulting firm. But hopes and dreams wouldn't give us a baby. For that, I needed cold, hard cash.

So I went to work. All day. All night. Busting my ass so I could offer her the world.

Only, in the process, I lost it all.

And, in my stupidity, she lost it all, too.

Money fixed exactly zero of my problems. I could buy anything I wanted.

Except her.

Never her.

"Roman," Kristen hissed, taking my hand and wrapping it around the edge of the plate. "Go!"

I closed my eyes, sucked in a breath, and did what I should have done years earlier.

I walked up the stairs to save my wife—and our family.

Only I didn't make it far.

A man greeted me at the top of the stairway.

"Fuck!" I yelled, my hands immediately going up in defense, french fries flying everywhere. I caught the plate at the last second as my eyes adjusted and I recognized the man.

Me.

"Fucking shit!" I shouted, taking in the floor-to-ceiling mirror that covered the entirety of the wall, including the one beside it that ran parallel to the two bedroom doors on one side of the landing.

It had most definitely not been there when I'd moved out, and frankly, it was scary as hell.

The door cracked, and Elisabeth's head poked out.

"What's wrong?" she asked, her cheeks still damp from crying.

I ignored her question and pointed to the mirror with the plate. "What the fucking hell is that?"

Her head twisted to the side, her lip curling with attitude as she answered, "A mirror."

"Okay, but why?"

She swung the door open and propped a shoulder on the jamb. "Well, originally, it was an effort to make this tiny hallway feel bigger. But it didn't exactly go as planned. Now, I just feel like I live in a fun house. I've been…"

I believe there were more words spoken after that, but the blood drained from my head in a rush down south.

She'd changed clothes. Elisabeth's sleep attire was much like her fancy daily wear. No frumpy old sweats for her. She slept in short, silky dresses, nightgowns, nighties. Whatever they were called, I loved them for a myriad of reasons. Including the way they showed her legs off and the ridiculously easy access they offered in the middle of the night. But, upon seeing her now, I remembered my favorite reason of all: They left absolutely nothing to the imagination. Everything, from the swell of her breasts to the curve of her hips, was outlined in spectacular fashion.

My eyes dropped to her nipples, which were peaking behind the fabric, and just as quickly, her arms came up to cross over them.

"Anyway," she said, "did you need something?"

Yes. You. Naked and calling my name. "You need to eat."

She rolled her eyes. "No. I need to sleep."

She started to close the door, but I caught it with my free hand.

"Why were you crying?" I asked.

"I wasn't."

"Bullshit." I took a step into the room, forcing her inside with me.

Her lips went thin as I kicked the door closed behind me.

"You need to leave," she contended while I moved past her to set the plate on her nightstand.

"Tell me why you were crying and I'll see what I can do about that," I lied.

She scoffed. "Oh, I don't know, Roman. You're a smart man. I'm sure you can figure this out without an explanation."

I glanced around the room. Not much had changed. Our wedding pictures were no longer covering the walls, but minus the khaki bedding that had been switched for a pink-and-white stripe, it all remained the same. Her closet door was wide open, shoes neatly organized over the floor, necklaces draped over hooks I'd mounted on the back of the

101

door.

When we'd bought the place, I'd promised her that I'd expand the closet for her. It was one of the many promises I'd broken to her.

"That guy, Jon. He mean something to you?" I asked, going to the window, peeking out just in time to see Kristen's car backing out of the driveway.

She laughed, but it held no humor. "That's seriously your first guess? After the day we've had, you guess I'm up here pining over Jon?"

I glanced back in her direction and cocked an eyebrow. "Is that a no?"

She released a frustrated groan, walked to the door, and snatched it open. "Leave."

I ignored her request and sat on the side of the bed. Resting my elbows on my knees, I interlocked my fingers and let them hang between my legs. "So, you're upset about the shit that went down at the police station today?"

She blinked for several seconds, her chest heavily rising and falling. She was about to explode, but sometimes, that was the only way to break a wall down.

"Lissy," I whispered, lighting the fuse.

Three.

Two.

One.

"No! I'm upset because this is my life!"

Boom!

She gave the door a hard shove, slamming it shut before marching over to me. Crossing her arms over her chest, she snapped, "Let's see. Where should I start?" She waited for a reply that wasn't going to come before she continued. "My day began in a police station, where I found out that someone might have pulled the old switch-a-roo on my embryos. Then I woke up a second time to find my ex-husband standing in my kitchen, drinking beer, and ordering dinner. Then he pinned me to a fucking couch, declaring his one hundred percent involvement." She paused and lifted two fingers in the air. "This being said *two* goddamn *years* after he'd checked out on me. Then his sister showed up, claiming to be *convincing* me of something, which he clearly seemed to be in on. Then my *friend* showed up because he's worried about me, and you marked me like a fucking fire hydrant. Now, here you are...standing in *my bedroom*, asking why *I'm* upset. Jesus Christ, Roman!" She threw her hands out to the sides. "Take your pick!"

She wasn't wrong.

All of that had happened.

But she'd left a lot of the details out.

After rising to my feet, I closed the distance between us. Her eyes went wide as I hooked an arm around her hips and pulled her off-balance so she crashed into my chest.

"See, my day went a little differently," I started gruffly. "I woke up this morning, after I'd spent the entire night trying to figure out how to get the woman I love to take money from me. She hates me, but I fucking hate the idea that I can't take care of her."

"I don't—" she started to interrupt, but I talked over her.

"I arrived at the police station, where I saw said woman, and I felt my heart beat for the very first time in two fucking

103

years."

Her mouth fell open, but when I cupped the back of her neck, she slammed it shut.

"*Then* I found out that some asshole I trusted enough to give my life savings to decided to sell *my* child to someone else. Yeah, I don't give a single fuck we used a sperm donor. I also don't give a damn that that child was in a petri dish when it was sold. That child is *ours*. Wherever the hell it might be right now." I paused for a breath, and she wisely remained quiet. "Then, upon hearing this news, you fell into my arms, clinging to me as if we'd never been apart. With *that*, Lis, my lungs inflated for the first time since I'd found you sitting on the couch with your bags packed around you. I walked out of that police station with you in my arms, shocked and pissed the fuck off, but I felt like someone had finally pressed play on my life again." I squeezed the back of her neck. "So, yeah, baby, you better believe I'm one hundred percent involved in *that*."

"Roman," she sighed, her stiff body finally starting to relax in my arms.

I kept going. "Then my annoying-ass sister showed up in order to convince you to keep at least some of the money I'd sent so I could get one single night of sleep where I didn't close my eyes and worry you needed something. I will *not* fucking apologize for that. That leads me to the part where a man I *do not know* showed up at your door, trying to steal that new beat in my heart and breath in my lungs, so damn straight I reacted. You aren't gonna get an apology from me about that, either. For fuck's sake, I called you my wife. I didn't beat the piss out of him. And believe me, the thought *did* cross my mind."

"Oh God," she cried, dropping her forehead to my chest. Her hand snaked up between us to rest on my pec.

After kissing the top of her head, I finished with, "So you were right about one thing. I am standing in your bedroom, asking why you are upset, because minus the bullshit going on with the cops, I see not one thing to be upset about. Also, I'm standing in your bedroom, staring at you in that fucking nightgown, and remembering how it looked the last time I took it off you."

Her head jerked up, her eyes wide and her cheeks sliding through the color spectrum of reds. "Don't," she warned, but it came out breathy.

"I won't," I assured as I slid my hands up her sides, allowing my thumbs to glide over the side of her breasts as I made my way up to her neck to cup her jaw. "Yet, anyway."

Her gaze darkened, and her hand at my chest closed, fisting my shirt. "This is crazy," she whined.

"It always was with us."

"I can't do this with you, Roman. Not again."

"Fine. Don't. But consider this your warning because…" I paused, turning us so I could back her to the bed. Bending so as not to lose the connection, I gently lowered her to the mattress and declared, "I'm checking back in."

She shook her head. "This isn't a hotel. You can't just check back in."

I battled the urge to kiss her.

To claim her.

To take back the woman who had always been mine.

Calling up every ounce of self-control I possessed, I released her, pushed off the bed, and headed to the door. After opening it, I shot her a smirk and said, "You're right. It's not. Otherwise, I wouldn't be sleeping on the fucking *couch*."

Her chin quivered as she smiled. God, she was scared to fucking death, and it broke me. But I wasn't letting go. Not again.

"It's gonna be okay. All of it," I promised.

A tear fell as she replied in a weak voice, "I'm not sure about that."

She was wrong. But I wasn't going to convince her of that right then.

"Try to eat and get some rest, okay?"

She nodded, wiping the wetness away from her cheeks.

I hated leaving her alone when she was struggling, but she needed the space, so begrudgingly, I walked away.

Then I yelled, "Son of a bitch!" when that goddamned man in the mirror scared the shit out of me for the second time.

And it was worth every second of the near heart attack when I heard Elisabeth's soft giggle from the other side of the door.

CHAPTER ELEVEN

ELISABETH

"**W**ake up, baby," I heard as I felt the hair being swept off my face.

It was him. Therefore, it had to be a dream.

It was a dream I'd had at least a dozen times.

However, once, it had been reality.

"Wake up, baby," he urged, sitting on the bed in the curve of my naked body. His back to my front, only a sheet dividing us. Thoughts of the night before flooded my mind—all of them starting and ending with Roman.

"Mmm," I purred, curling around him. Looping my arms at his waist, I groaned when I came in contact with his clothes. My sore, well-used body was still aching from the night before, but I was ready for more. "Why are you dressed?" I complained, teasingly patting him down, paying special attention to his zipper while searching for the length hiding behind it.

Just as I found it, he caught my wrist and pulled it away. "We need to talk."

It wasn't spoken in a tone that said, We need to talk so we can figure out where to get more condoms and then stay in the bed for the rest of the day—and maybe forever.

It was spoken in a tone that said, We need to talk because I'm married and need to get home to my wife.

I was suddenly more awake than ever.

"What's wrong?" I asked, sitting up, dragging the sheet with me.

He was no less gorgeous the next morning, but the mischievous glint in his silver eyes was now filled with worry. It was all wrong for the man who had proposed only hours earlier.

"How ya feeling?" he asked, pushing to his feet and pacing the room.

"Good," I drawled suspiciously.

He stopped moving and looked over at me. "Not sick or anything?"

I tilted my head in question and replied, "Nope. Little thirsty. Little hungover. But overall pretty good."

Scrubbing the top of his buzzed head, he breathed, "Oh, thank God."

This did not relax me in the least.

"Roman, what's going on?"

He swallowed hard then went back to pacing a path in my carpet. "I fucked up, Lis."

My already racing heart came to a screeching halt.

He'd fucked up.

Oh God.

"How?" I had no idea where the courage to ask had come from, because no one wanted to be rejected by a man who they'd fallen in love with. And that was exactly what had happened. I'd thought I had known it as he'd made love to me on the floor just inside my apartment and then again a few hours later in my bed. But, right then, staring down the barrel of losing him, I knew.

Roman Leblanc was it for me.

And he'd fucked up.

He looked at me with terrified eyes and announced, "I was drunk."

I was going to be sick. I could feel it in my stomach. I wasn't going to be able to hold it together much longer.

"Roman, I'm about to have a panic attack, so if you could just speak in full thoughts and spit this shit out, I'd really appreciate it. What did you do?"

He balled his hands into fists, planting them on his hips as he confessed, "It was lamb!"

My head snapped back. "What?"

"I'm so fucking sorry. I've been freaking out all morning." He started pacing again. "I searched your fridge and pantry, and there's not a piece of lamb anywhere. Are you allergic? Please tell me it's not a delayed reaction. Shit. Damn. Fuck. Do we need to go to the hospital?" He gripped the back of his neck and stared at me. "Oh God, please don't tell me it's a religious thing and I knowingly fed you lamb."

My breath became lodged in my throat.

This smart, funny, and beautiful man was freaking out because he'd told me that the gyros were beef. He had a conscience so strong that it had woken him early in the morning

109

and sent him scouring through my pantry.

The guilt was painted all over his face.

If I'd had any doubts left about Roman, that was the exact moment they vanished.

I was hopeless to stop the tears from falling.

"Say something," he whispered in absolute horror.

"Yes," I said on a half cry, half laugh.

His eyebrows pinched together. "Yes, allergic, or yes, religious?"

I sob-laughed again. "Yes, I'll marry you."

His whole body startled, and his mouth gaped open.

I quickly amended, "I mean, if the offer's still on the table."

"Oh my God," he gasped. "Are you serious?"

I nodded, wiping my cheeks and climbing to my knees.

He rushed across my bedroom faster than any non-Olympic athlete could move. Slamming into me, he wrapped his arms around my shoulders and lifted me off the bed.

"Holy shit," he breathed, planting random kisses on the top of my hair and the side of my face. "Say it again."

"Yes, I'll marry you."

"Jesus," he whispered. "I thought I was going to lose you."

I giggled. "Over lamb?"

He pinched my side. "I spent forty-five minutes searching the Internet for lamb allergies. I even held a mirror under your nose to make sure you were still breathing."

I burst out laughing as he put me back on the bed. "For the record, I eat lamb. I'm just not a fan of it in anything but a gyro."

"Noted." He pressed his lips to mine in a reverent kiss.

Then he leaned away and smiled, declaring, "You're gonna be Elisabeth—with an S—Leblanc by the end of the day."

I smiled back. "Leblanc with a capital or lowercase B?"

He smirked. "Does it matter?"

I struggled to get rid of my smile, but the best I could do was cover it with my hand. "Yes, it matters. Our lives together hang in the balance of this question right here. Right now."

He chewed on his bottom lip, trying to cover his own shit-eating grin. "Lowercase."

I sucked in a deep breath and then took the biggest risk of my entire life.

And I did it knowing that it wasn't really a risk at all.

Because, regardless of my answer, I would love this man for the rest of my life.

"Okay, then. Roman Leblanc—with a lowercase B—let's get married."

I kept my eyes closed as I stretched. "What time is it?" I asked, rolling to my side and curling around him.

"Jesus," he mumbled as I felt him touch the spaghetti strap of my nightie. His thumb grazed my skin as it trailed down between my breasts. My nipples peaked in anticipation.

But then he moved the fabric to cover me. *Wrong direction.*

I groaned in disappointment when consciousness finally pulled me from my dream world.

My eyes flashed open, and I found him staring down at my chest as he righted the material over my exposed breast.

I bolted upright and scrambled across the bed, dragging the sheet with me. "Wh-what are you doing here?" I asked, memories of the night before still lost in the early morning fog.

He twisted his lips, his eyes darkening as they slid to my hands, which were clutching the sheet, then back again. "Our legal team will be here in fifteen minutes. I thought you might like to get dressed."

With that, the world came crashing back down around me. My body sagged, and my heart wrenched. I would have rather stayed in bed all day and forget that I needed a legal team in the first place.

"Okay," I forced out.

Before I knew it, his hand was at the back of my neck, dragging me toward him. It wasn't rough, but it was demanding. He tucked my face into his neck and shifted so my chest was crushed against his side.

I didn't fight. I'd just woken up and didn't have it in me. Or so I told myself as I nuzzled closer.

"It's gonna be okay, Lissy," he whispered into my hair, his lips sealing the promise with a kiss on my crown.

"Okay," I mumbled, doing my best to tamp the overwhelming anxiety down.

"It's just a meeting with Whit and Kaplin to see what our options are."

"Okay," I agreed again.

One hand remained at the back of my neck, and he folded the other arm around my shoulders, holding me so tight that it was as if he could keep me from falling apart. And this was Roman; he might have been the only one who could. It was his superpower as far as I was concerned.

"I'm right here. One hundred percent," he said, continuing with the reassurance.

I continued with the noncommittal declarations of acceptance. "Okay."

"You want some coffee?" he asked before kissing the top of my head again.

I shouldn't have liked that as much as I did.

There were reasons Roman and I were no longer together. I needed to focus on those and not the desire to crawl into his lap and ride out the rest of the day in his arms.

Drawing in a breath, I forced myself to my feet. "I need to get dressed, but yeah, I'd love coffee. The creamer is—"

"In the cabinet. Powder. I remember," he said, scrubbing his hands over his...

Jeans?

"Where'd you get clothes?" I asked, heading to my closet—the one that used to be his.

"Seth. He dropped off my car this morning, too."

I turned and looked through the blinds to see a brand-spanking-new Range Rover sitting in my driveway. And, for reasons I didn't understand, just the sight of that fucking car sent ice through my veins. This wasn't the past where Roman was mine and he woke me up and held me in the morning while I calmed myself from the stress of the day.

This was the present where Roman had checked out on me, we'd gotten a divorce, and he'd started up a multimillion-dollar company while I'd struggled to breathe.

Anger was a worthless emotion, but bitterness and resentment were impossible to ignore.

I snapped the blinds shut as I sniped, "That's a far cry

from the broke-down Honda you left in."

I couldn't see him, but I felt the air crackle around us. Then, just as quickly, everything fell flat. Glancing over my shoulder, I saw him moving toward me—fast.

His chest hit my back at the same time that fucking hand of his slid into my hair.

My body responded immediately, spiking my pulse and flushing my cheeks.

With a gentle tug, he sent chills spreading over my skin as he pulled my head back. Our eyes met. Mine were wide. His were feral.

I couldn't breathe.

I couldn't talk.

I couldn't even think.

Not with his hard body at my back, his breath on my skin, and his mouth inches away from mine.

His hand squeezed my waist as it slowly glided up my stomach, stopping just below the round of my breasts. His thumb gently swept the swell before disappearing.

My lids drooped at the contact, and my head fell back against his shoulder. As I gave him my weight, he shifted his hand from my neck around to my throat.

"There she is. My sweet Lissy," he praised softly.

As much as I needed to keep my distance, I knew it was a futile. I'd never been able to stay away from him.

And that obviously hadn't changed.

He was amazing in bed, and I was positive that hadn't changed, either.

I hadn't been with anyone since our divorce. And, the year before it, I had been pregnant, recovering, or lost in despair. Sex hadn't been very high on our list of priorities.

Maybe we could remedy this now. At least physically.

Trusting him with my body doesn't mean trusting him with my heart.

Or so I told myself during my "it's okay to sleep with your ex-husband" mental pep talk.

It was a successful one too, because seconds later, I threw in the towel with a silent, *Fuck it.*

Arching my back, I pressed my ass against his hips and circled. I heard his groan just as I closed my eyes and set aim on his mouth.

Only he didn't meet me halfway.

He didn't meet me at *all.*

He released me and walked away, saying, "I wish I could say the same about your car. It was a piece of shit when we bought it. It's worse now. You need something new."

I blinked.

What had just happened?

Oh, that's right. I got shut the fuck down by my ex-husband after he'd basically fondled my boobs and pulled my hair.

Roman Leblanc strikes again.

"Get out!" I growled. (Yes, growled. Apparently, it was contagious.)

"Yep," he replied like I'd asked him to pass the salt. He never looked back as he headed out the door, but he paused just before closing it long enough to call over his shoulder, "After our meeting, I have to hit the office for an hour or so today. I'll bring back dinner."

He would *not* be bringing dinner back that night because I'd be staying at the dodgy motel two counties over. I didn't inform him of this information by chasing him down the stairs the way I would have liked. Instead, I took a shower, brushed my teeth, and got dressed, all the while cursing my libido.

CHAPTER TWELVE

ROMAN

Our attorneys had nothing. Not. One. Fucking. Thing. The cops weren't allowed to tell us the name of the other couple involved so we could deal with it privately. We had to sit on our hands and wait for the APD to feed us more information as it became available—*if* it became available.

I was beyond frustrated by this news, but Elisabeth was notably distraught. My attempts to soothe her only made it worse.

She was probably pissed at me for having shot her down in the bedroom when she'd all but offered me her naked body on a silver platter. But *fuck*. I'd had fifteen minutes before Whit and Kaplin arrived. There was no way, the first time I had her in what felt like an eternity—but probably calculated closer to three years—it was going to be in a quickie against the closet wall. Though, after that little grind down with her ass, I'd been tempted.

After our attorneys gave us a full briefing and left, Elisabeth locked herself away in the second bedroom, stating that she had work to do. She probably did, but the way she'd said it was more like, *Get the fuck out of my house.*

I gave her that because I did, in fact, have work to do. And the sooner I got to the office and got it done, the sooner I could get back over to her place and finish what she had started.

It was a rare day when I didn't wear a suit to the office. I hated that shit, all stiff and as comfortable as a cardboard straitjacket, but if I wanted people to believe I belonged behind the massive desk in the corner office, I had to look the part.

After my morning, though, I hadn't felt like going back to my apartment before heading in for a couple of hours. So, in a pair of jeans that were barely held together by a thread and a T-shirt that wasn't much better, I exited the elevator at Leblanc Industries.

"Mr. Leblanc?" my secretary said with surprise.

Just as fast, a man repeated, "Mr. Leblanc?"

I stopped as he moved toward me. "Can I help you?"

He was around my age, well-built, and exuding authority, so it didn't surprise me in the least when he flipped a badge my way. "Agent Heath Light, DEA. Can we have a word in private?" He tucked a manila folder under his arm in order to extend a hand.

I often had members of the force in the office; I made bulletproof material for a living. But, with my luck, Simon Wells had sent this guy by to harass me into selling him a load of Rubicon.

I shook his outstretched hand and said, "Listen, I'm really busy today. Can you make an appointment for next week? I'd be happy to have a sit-down and discuss numbers with—"

"This is *personal*, Roman."

Personal.

Roman.

The fuck?

I arched an eyebrow as I gave him a slow nod, calling to my secretary, "Hold my calls."

I led the way to my office as he silently followed behind me. Once inside, he didn't get much more talkative. I sat in my chair and fired my computer up as he walked around, inspecting the pictures hanging around the room.

He pointed to one on the wall and said, "She's cute."

I rocked back in my chair and replied, "She's my *sister*."

"You still caught up on your ex?" he questioned like the ballsy motherfucker he clearly was.

I sat up, propped my elbows on my desk, and ignored his question. "What can I help you with today, Agent Light?"

He tipped his chin in my direction. "Lucked out. Your secretary told me you were out for the day."

"I *am* out for the day," I corrected. "So, if you could speed this up, I'd be much obliged."

He finally moved to the chair in front of my desk and sat. "Good. This way, it'll be easier to explain away that I was *never* here."

"I'm sorry?"

He slid a photo from his envelope but kept it facedown. "Roman, I'm here on a *very unofficial* capacity today. You

119

got me?"

I narrowed my eyes, my gaze going to the photo I couldn't make out. "I got you," I replied skeptically.

"I also need your word that you're not gonna go off half-cocked and get yourself killed. That would make my life *extremely* messy right about now."

"Get to the fucking point," I demanded, quickly losing my patience with the vague bullshit.

"That your word?"

I shrugged. "It's gonna have to be. The only other ones I got for you are: Get the hell out of my office."

He stared at me for a minute before his face split in a grin. "I hear you and your woman got some news yesterday."

Now, *that* got my attention.

I steepled my fingers under my chin. "We did. You got anything in that magic envelope of yours that might be helpful to me?"

He grinned again and then demanded, "Your word."

"Never seen you in my life. I spent the day at home with Elisabeth, reuniting our marriage between the sheets."

He chuckled. "Works for me." Sliding a grainy, black-and-white surveillance picture across the desk, he said, "Walter Noir. Bad guy. And, when I say bad guy, I mean bad. Fucking. Guy. We've been keeping tabs on him for the last three years. He's the big name in drugs in the city right now. His army is strong, but worse than that, they're tight. Nobody in or out without Noir's personal approval. He's into some deep shit. You owe that man money, he's got tricks that make the old-school mob look like child's play. The blood on his hands could forge rivers."

I set the photo back on my desk. "And you're telling me this why?"

He pulled more pictures from the envelope and then slid the bottom one my way. "That's his wife Clare."

I could only see the side of her face, but that was all I needed in order to make out the wide black-and-blue bruise covering her cheek.

"Jesus," I muttered.

"That was taken outside of her gym eight months ago. It's the only place he allows her to go. The bastard keeps her on a tight leash." He passed me another picture. "This one was taken five months ago."

In this image, she was looking straight at the camera, tears flowing down her cheeks and dark bruises peeking from the neck of her tank top.

"This one was three months ago." Another image of the thin, blond, battered woman.

He started to slide another my way, but I lifted my hand in the air.

"Enough. I got it. Get to the part where you give me something helpful."

He stood and bent over my desk, slapping a picture down into the center. Then he stabbed his index finger down on the back of a little, blond head in the woman's arms and changed my entire life with one sentence. "That is the child who may or may not be your daughter."

I shot to my feet, the chair rolling from under me and slamming into the shelves that lined the wall behind me. After snatching the picture off the desk, I brought it up to my face for a closer inspection. It was nothing but a head full of white curls, but I couldn't tear my eyes away.

"Are you sure?" I asked.

"Am I sure it's your kid? No. Do I think it's a strong possibility based on the asshole who's involved? Yes."

I snatched my desk phone up and lifted it to my ear, but his hand slammed down on the base, hanging it up.

"What the fuck are you doing?"

"I'm calling the cops…or shit, my attorney…or, Christ, *someone*."

"I *am* the cops, Roman. And I assure you there is not one fucking thing we can do to help you here. If we could, I'd be off doing it rather than standing here, risking my job."

"Jesus, shit!" I yelled, raking my hand through my hair. "What the hell am I supposed to do here?" I snatched a picture of the bruised woman off the desk and lifted it his way. "He doing that to the kid?"

He cut his eyes away. "Tessa. Her name's Tessa, and I don't know."

"Bullshit! You know."

"No. I really don't fucking know. But even if he isn't. He *will*. Eventually."

"Goddamn it!" I slammed my fist down.

"You cannot go to the authorities with this."

"Then what the fuck do you expect me to do!" I yelled so loud the windows rattled.

His eyes hollowed into dark, treacherous pits. "I expect you to get *her* out."

"Kidnapping?" I laughed humorlessly. "Fan-fuck-ing-tastic idea."

"Not the kid." He once again stabbed his finger down

on my desk. Only, this time, it landed on the woman. "*Her.*"

"What?" I asked in disbelief.

"She's the key to this entire investigation."

"Fuck your investigation," I shot back.

"That woman holds all the answers. Legally, she's the mother of that child. She can submit to DNA testing on herself and the girl. We find out the kid's not hers, we have ourselves a case no judge could ignore. Court order on Walter Noir plus her testimony on all the bullshit she's seen over the years. That man's done."

He made it sound so easy. But just the fact that he was standing in my office told me it was the impossible. I had a sneaking suspicion that I was about to become the DEA's sacrificial lamb.

"And what if she doesn't submit to DNA? She might be on a tight leash, but what if she doesn't want to get away? You'd be throwing me into the line of fire, keeping your hands clean, *and* getting your case. No fucking thanks."

His jaw turned to granite, and his hands flexed at his sides. "You get her away from that man, I have not one single doubt that she will sing like a fucking bird. She's scared, Leblanc. But, from what we can tell, she is *not* involved in his shit. She's just a victim. Best thing that ever happened to her is that lab tech spilling it on the doctor and Noir. She needs an out, and I need you to get off your ass, get creative, and give that to her."

"And how exactly do you expect me to do this?" I asked, my voice thick with sarcasm as I walked around the desk and settled on the corner. "Just walk into the lion's den and take his woman *and* his child?"

He crossed his arms over his chest and ignored my question. "The second best thing that happened to her was her embryo being switched with *yours*."

I scoffed and blankly gazed out the window. "Right."

"Leblanc, I've done my research on you. Prior military. Infantry. Two purple hearts and a boatload of men who respect the fuck out of you. You're smart. Fucking loaded, yet you live in a shithole apartment in the garage of an even bigger shithole house. You're charitable but run your business with a heavy hand. You wanted to be a family man, but that wasn't in the cards. Now, your ex-wife hates you, but you've been making some headway there in the last twenty-four hours, yeah?"

I pushed to my feet and took a step toward him. "You been watching me?"

He didn't hesitate to grin as he said, "Since the moment that snitch said your name."

"Right."

"Right," he replied, moving back to his chair, grabbing his envelope before riffling through it. "If there was ever a man who could handle this, it's you. You have the resources. So fucking use them. Get eyes on Clare, find a good time, and then make your approach. Be gentle. She spooks easy. She needs help, Roman. Make her understand that you can give her that." He pulled one last picture out and set it facedown on my desk. Then he passed the envelope my way. "That's as much information as I could get on her. Her address. Schedule. Gym location. All of her background. It should be a good start for whoever you hire. And should you need someone you can trust, there's the name of a protection agency in there as well. It's run by a man named Leo James. He used to be DEA. He mainly does personal security now, but you give him a call, drop my name, and he'll take care of you."

I nodded though I had no idea what I was agreeing to, but I took the envelope from his hands, knowing I had to do something.

Heath walked to the door. Then he stopped and looked back at me. "I don't think I need to remind you about the urgency of this situation, but I'm gonna do it anyway. Do *not* sit on this, Leblanc. Get on the phone, throw some money at people, and get that woman and *your daughter* out of there."

My body jerked at his definitive use of the term *your daughter*.

"Saw pictures of Elisabeth at the police station," he added, lifting his chin to the photo he'd left facedown on my desk. "It's obvious."

I immediately snatched it up and...

"Holy shit," I gasped.

But there was no way to deny it.

The oxygen drained from the room and the only thing left was a photo of a child with blond ringlets and a face I'd recognize anywhere. I'd seen it in my dreams nearly every night as we'd struggled through infertility.

She was Elisabeth's.

Absolutely. One hundred percent. Without question.

By the time I tore my gaze up, Heath was gone.

I didn't do as he'd instructed. I didn't pick the phone up and make any calls.

Instead, I grabbed my keys and stormed from the office.

One destination in mind.
And it wasn't home.

CHAPTER THIRTEEN

CLARE

'd cried myself to sleep the night before. That wasn't anything new. However, this time, I did it in Walt's arms. I'd had no other choice. He hadn't let me out of his sight since he'd stormed into Luke's office, yanked me into his arms, and hugged me as if he hadn't seen me in decades rather than minutes. He glared at Luke only for a second before he guided me, with Tessa in my arms, out to a waiting car in the parking lot. The police were swarming, but no one could touch Walter Noir.

The entire day had been mind-boggling. I'd expected Walt to lose his shit that I'd spoken with the police—even if they had been the ones speaking to me. But the minute we arrived home, he gave me the kind, gentle, and understanding man I'd fallen in love with while we had been dating. I knew now that that man didn't exist, but as my heart struggled to beat with the newest gaping hole, I'd never been so grateful for the façade.

The moment he got me behind closed doors, he guided me up to the office, where he produced two sets of DNA results. My name at the top of one, his at the top of the other, Tessa's on both. I stared at them as he crouched in front of me, holding my hand and explaining that the police had approached him weeks earlier about the possibility of a lab error. He'd refused the DNA test because he'd feared they were using it as a ploy to once and for all get a legally surrendered sample of his DNA.

For an average man, handing the police department a sample of DNA would be no big deal and the results would end up in a dusty box in the evidence room at the end of an investigation.

For a man like Walter Noir—a money-laundering, drug-dealing, murdering low life with ties to people so bad that the government didn't even have them on a radar yet—handing his DNA over was the equivalent of a life sentence. I didn't know everything Walt was involved in, but I knew enough. I was positive there was a case file the size of a library on him, and the cops were begging for a way to tie him to it all.

So he told me that he'd had his own DNA tests performed at a private lab to ease his mind, and he hadn't told me because he hadn't wanted to upset me.

As if he'd ever cared if he upset me before.

Still in a state of shock, I listened to him while tracing my finger over Tessa's name, but never Noir. And, for the briefest of seconds, I wished that the results read differently. I couldn't live without Tessa, but if it meant she wasn't

Walt's, I could die with a whole heart.

I nodded and told him that I understood.

But I understood nothing.

The truth was masked by a million lies.

The only thing I knew for sure was that Walt's "results" were worth about as much as the paper they were printed on, based on nothing more than the fact that they had come from his hands.

I wasn't sure if the cop's story held any validity, but I wasn't in any position to ask questions.

At least, not yet.

Tessa was mine no matter what a piece of paper read.

My job as her mother was to keep her safe, and that didn't end because of genetics—or the lack thereof.

Unfortunately, that job became exponentially more difficult the very next day.

Tessa and I were playing with sidewalk chalk on the driveway when a black Range Rover stopped at the front gate.

It wasn't unusual for Walt's men to show up and let themselves in, but they all had their own code to get inside, so it caught my attention when the man put the car in park and exited his vehicle.

"Mrs. Noir?" he called, moving toward the bars of the gate.

He was big, his shoulders broad, his hair perfectly styled, but he was wearing a pair of tattered jeans and a vintage T-shirt that had to be older than I was. And it should be known he was wearing it *really* well. But there was no way a man like that could afford a car like the one he rolled up in.

He had to be one of Walt's men. I didn't care what the old slogan said—crime definitely paid.

"Did you forget your code?" I called out, using my hand to shield the sun from my eyes.

"I…ah… Yeah. Any chance you could let me in?"

Not if I value my life. I strolled closer, figuring he must be new. "Sorry, man. You know the rules. Call one of the guys."

"I…don't have my phone," he replied. "Any chance I can borrow yours?"

I barked a laugh. Clearly, he didn't value *his* life. I was off-limits to all of Walt's guys. This conversation alone was borderline dangerous.

I stopped in front of the gate and shook my head. "What's your name? I'll text Brock and see if he can help you out."

I was pulling my phone from my pocket when it happened. His hand darted through the bars, and he grabbed my forearm and slammed me into the gate.

My heart lurched as my face pressed against the metal bars.

"Listen to me," he demanded in a rough and scary whisper.

My eyes darted back to Tessa, who was still thankfully focused on her sidewalk chalk Picasso of Dora the Explorer. "Let me go! He'll kill you if he sees you touching me!" I said quietly so as not to startle her.

His voice was low and desperate as he said, "My name is Roman Leblanc. My wife and I did in vitro fertilization at Peach City Reproductive Center three years ago. The police recently informed us that our embryos might have been switched. And I'm here because I believe they were switched with yours, and I also believe your husband is responsible."

My lungs burned at the same time my nose began to sting. What was a nightmare within a nightmare called? Because I was currently living one.

"You're wrong." I lied. "Let me go." I attempted to shake his hand off, but his grip tightened.

"I also believe you, much like my wife and I, are an innocent party in this. I've heard about your husband, Clare. I know he puts his hands on you. On her."

As I struggled against his hold on me, Tessa decided to finally look up.

"Mama!" she cried, and his hold on me momentarily loosened at the sound.

I took the opportunity to yank my arm from his grasp, but just as quickly, he caught the front of my shirt.

"I'm a man of resources, Clare. I can save you. I can save Tessa," he swore, his desperate, gray eyes shining the truth. He believed he could do it.

I believed something a little different. "You're about to get us both killed! Let me go. Walk away. And forget this address. *Now*," I spat back at him.

Tessa careened into my legs, sobbing. I patted her hair down and held Roman's stare. "Shhh... Mama's okay. The scary man was just leaving."

His face was stone, but I saw the wince before he could hide it.

"Leave before he sees you here," I begged.

He shook his head. "Two choices. You pick her up and

get in my car right this fucking second. Or, the next time you see me, I will be taking her *without* you."

The blood roared in my ears, and my vision tunneled.

I'd spent my life protecting her from one asshole. I sure as hell wasn't going to allow another to take her from me.

Years of pain and fear all joined forces in the span of a second, igniting my adrenaline into a fiery rage. My fist flew through the bars of the gate, slamming into his face as I shrieked, "You will not touch my daughter! Ever."

Surprise registered on his face as he dodged my second scrambled blow. "Then help me get her away from him!" he implored. "I'm here to help you, Clare. I swear on my life I would never let anything happen to her. *Or you.* Just open the fucking gate and get in my goddamn car." Anguish filled his voice, but again, even through my fury, I knew he was being honest.

But Walt had held that same truth in his eyes once, and look where that had gotten me.

His hand was still wrapped in the front of my shirt, and even with the adrenaline fueling me, I was no match for him, so I drew in a breath and used the only resource I possessed.

It was wrong, and it felt filthy to utilize it on what seemed like a decent man, but much like the rest of my life, I was out of options. Opening my mouth, I screamed Walt's name at the top of my lungs.

His eyes grew wide as he started shaking his head. "No!" he growled. Then his anger morphed into pleas. "Come with me. Please." His eyes flashed to the door behind me.

Tears rolled down my cheeks as I waited for my dark

knight to appear, swoop me off my feet, and carry me back to the dungeons of Hell.

"Clare, please," he said, digging into his back pocket and retrieving his wallet. Without releasing me, he flipped it open and shoved it in my face. "This is my wife. Look at her!"

It took a second for my eyes to focus, but when they did, I wasn't sure I'd be able to see anything else ever again.

Tessa's eyes.

Tessa's nose.

Tessa's hair.

Tessa's smile.

"No," I breathed.

With the exception of my eyes, I'd always thought Tessa looked like me. But, with one glance at that woman, I realized just how wrong I'd been.

"Her name's Elisabeth, and she's a good woman. I scared you. I'm sorry. But please hear me when I say I *can* help you. And if you don't believe me, fine. Give me the DNA. Get the police involved. They can help you. I'm not here to take her away from you. I'm here to get you *both* someplace safe."

I couldn't have answered if I'd tried.

But I never even got the chance.

"Fuck!" Roman barked, letting me go and then hauling ass back to his car.

Walter must have finally shown up to save me—from a man who was actually trying to *save* me.

No.

No.

No.

No.
No.
No.
No!

CHAPTER FOURTEEN

ELISABETH

I spent the day finding things to do in order to keep my mind off...well, my life.

I returned phone calls from clients who had zero intention of actually buying a house. Replied to emails from other clients who were concerned about why their overpriced, smelly house had been on the market for over twenty-four hours. And then I had lunch with Jon where I had the unfortunate task of informing him that Roman was back in my life. At least temporarily.

He smiled. Lied and said he was happy for me. I felt like a total heel. After a quick hug in front of a sandwich shop, I watched a good friend walk away for what I hoped wouldn't be the last time.

Roman was in a mood when he got home. Unfortunately, so was I, considering my house was not his home and he had used a key, which I had not given him, to get in the front door. He'd at least had the good manners to toss it in the key basket when he'd slammed the door behind himself. I made a mental note to remove it from his key ring before kicking him out.

"What are you doing here?" I snapped, rising off the couch as he marched to the back door to let a tap-dancing Loretta outside.

It should be said that she was not the best guard dog.

"Change of plans. I'll have Seth deliver dinner again. Figure out what you want. I need a shower," he said before heading to the stairs.

"Um, maybe we should try that again? What are you doing here?" I asked his back while following him up.

"Anything but Chinese and I'll be cool."

"Roman," I called. I was hot on his heels as he walked past my bedroom door and yanked the door to the hall closet open.

"Actually, I could do a good burger."

"Roman!" I finally yelled when it was clear he had no intentions of answering my question.

He lifted his gaze to mine and said, "What?"

"What?" I repeated, dumbfounded.

"Yeah. *What*, Lis? You got something to say? Let's hear it, because right now, I need a shower, a beer, and, if it's good with you, a fucking burger."

Roman was officially off his rocker, so I gave it to him gently. Which meant I only used minimal sarcasm when I *gave* it to him.

"Okay. Well, then you better hurry home and get on that."

"That's what I'm trying to do." He bent down to the bottom of the closet and retrieved a gym bag that was busting at the seams.

He's leaving. Praise the Lord!

He squeezed my hip as he walked past me…

Directly.

Into.

My.

Room.

"What are you doing?" I asked a little louder than I had planned, but it was still below a shriek, so I chalked it up as a huge demonstration of self-restraint.

He tossed the bag into the corner by the bed, and it slid across the hardwood until coming to rest against the wall. "Jesus Christ, Lis. We *just* discussed this."

"No. What we discussed was you going home to *your* house, taking a shower, drinking a beer, and ordering a burger. I'm not sure why I'd have to agree to said burger seeing as how I *won't* be eating dinner with you. But, if you need that approval, you got it!"

His eyes narrowed and the muscles in his sexy, sexy jaw began to tick as he ground out, "I know you heard me say I was checking back in last night."

I threw my arms out to my sides. "Still not a hotel!"

He sucked in a hard breath, his chest expanding, and just like his jaw, it was sexy squared. "I had a shit day, Lis," he warned, scrubbing a hand over his smooth chin. "I'm not coming home to more shit. So check your attitude before I check it for you."

My mouth fell open as I gasped. "You did *not* just

threaten me."

"For fuck's sake," was all he said before he was on the move.

And, as it seemed he only had one speed when he was pissed, he did it *fast*.

One of his hands went to my ass, the other into the back of my hair, and he had me pinned against the wall beside the door before I could even protest.

My body heated from head to toe as his fingers in my hair curled into a fist like he had done so many other times over the last twenty-four hours.

It was clear I needed to either shave my head or find a way to amputate his arms, because the sparks that fired off inside me had become progressively more intense each time. I feared I'd spontaneously combust if there was a next time.

"Roman," I breathed, though I should have been fighting against him.

Coulda. Shoulda. Woulda.

"I'm not fucking leaving. There is a shitstorm brewing around us, and I'm gonna take care of it. But, in that, I'm gonna take care of you, too. You gotta trust me on that, Lis. I fucked up in the past. I thought I was doing the right thing, but I see now that I wasn't. I'll explain that to you later. But do not for one second think that you are going to melt for me the way you did yesterday, again last night, and then again this morning after two fucking years and then you're gonna take it away."

"I don't know what you're talking about," I said, feigning innocence, though I knew exactly what he was talking about. I had melted for him. I just wasn't ready to acknowledge it. Not even to myself, and certainly not to him.

He twisted his lips. Then he proved his point by using my ass to grind me against his thickening length, which drew a moan from my throat.

"You feel it between us," he declared.

"Roman, you're very well…um…endowed," I informed in a sugary-sweet tone before finishing with a snap. "Of course I fucking feel it." It was a last-ditch effort to keep from falling under his spell.

It failed.

He grinned arrogantly and gave my ass a squeeze.

I moaned, and this time, I ground into *him*.

He dropped his elbow to the wall. "Christ, Lis."

That small victory allowed me to take some of the power back. I couldn't lie: I wanted Roman. I'd been physically and mentally strung out all afternoon as I'd sat on the couch, waiting for him to come back while equally hoping he didn't.

But the fact remained. He did come back. And, now, he had me pinned against the wall, only two layers of clothes separating me from what I knew would be an incredible night of ecstasy. And, through all of this, he hadn't kissed me yet.

And I couldn't bring myself to care.

"Fine. If we're gonna do this, we're doing it my way. One night. You leave when we're done."

"Done?" He laughed. And not just a chuckle. I'm talking an all out belly laugh like I'd taken up a side gig as a stand-up comedienne.

"I'm serious," I defended.

"You're a lot of things. But serious is not one of them. I get inside you, I'll have my ring back on your finger by tomorrow night."

Oh, hell no! We are not going back down that road.

I gave him a hard shove. "You will *not*. Don't even think about it. That is not what this is about."

He smirked. "Don't worry, baby. I'm not proposing."

That mildly relaxed me.

Well, until his lips descended upon mine and he said, "But you'll still say yes," a half second before taking my mouth.

Oh God.

Yes.

Without hesitation, I opened like the desperate woman I was, welcoming him home. His tongue greedily swirled with mine, and I circled my arms around his neck, taking him deeper, my nipples tingling as they met his chest.

After releasing my hair, he moved his hand down to the other side of my ass and lifted me off the floor. I took the cue and wrapped my legs around his waist. My dress gave way and his straining hard-on made contact with my lace-covered core, forcing a cry from my lips.

It had been too long.

Too long without him.

Too long since I'd reached for the toy tucked into the back of my bedside table.

Too long since I'd dropped my finger between my legs in the shower.

Part of that was because it paled in comparison to the real thing.

The other part being that I couldn't close my eyes without imagining it was *him*.

No matter how much I'd told myself to let him go, he was always in the forefront of my mind.

But there he was, in the flesh, carrying me to a bed that had once been ours, and I was ready to let him take me in any and every way he wanted.

He set me on the edge of the mattress and then followed me down. His hands landed on either side of my head, his mouth still moving with a practiced ease over mine.

I kept my legs around his hips, locking my feet at the ankle and using them as leverage to circle myself against him.

"Fuck, baby," he grumbled into my mouth.

I made fast work of peeling his shirt over his head then sat up off the bed long enough for him to tug the zipper at the back of my dress down. He didn't delay in pulling it over my head.

As much as I'd lied to myself about what was going to happen if he showed back up tonight, deep down, I'd known. And it was that knowledge that left me sitting in front of him in only a pair of black lace panties and a matching bra that were not only beautiful, but the pattern was so wide that it was damn near invisible. Everything from my nipples to my slit was on display.

With an approving rumble, he raked his eyes over me. Licking his lips, he pushed me back flat and sank to his knees between my legs, which were hanging over the side of the bed.

"Repeat after me," he ordered, gliding his hands up my

chest, gripping both of my breasts, and then smoothing his palms back down my stomach.

I moaned, arching off the bed while seductively sliding my bare foot up his side.

"This is not one night. You will not shut down on me. I get you're scared. We'll figure out that part later. After I make you come, fast and hard against my mouth. After I shower. After I drink a beer. After my burger. But before I fuck you."

Drunk on the promise of feeling him between my legs, I would have agreed to anything, but something he'd said required discussion.

Brazenly, I sat up and threaded a hand into the top of his hair, using it to pull him back to my mouth for a toe-curling kiss. When I released his mouth, I corrected him. "*After* you fuck me."

"No," he replied firmly.

I had no choice but to move my assault farther south. Dragging my tongue down the corded muscles of his neck, I pushed my argument. "We'll talk *after*, Roman."

His hand moved into the back of my hair again, and it wasn't helping his case in the least. My entire nervous system lit up like the New York City power grid.

And then the most incredible thing happened.

For the first time since he'd come back into my life, Roman Leblanc didn't argue.

"Okay. *After*," he rumbled, thrusting a hand into my panties then pressing a single finger inside me.

"Yes," I panted against his shoulder while spreading my legs wider.

"Take off your bra, baby," he ordered, giving my hair a gentle pull and adding another finger.

"Oh God," I cried at the beautiful bite at my scalp.

"Off," he repeated, guiding my mouth back to his.

As his tongue stroked mine, I obeyed and unclasped the back of my bra, allowing it to fall from my arms.

I groaned in remorse when his hand left my hair, but then I groaned for a different reason as it landed on my breast. I rolled my shoulders back to encourage him to take more. I didn't have the biggest breasts, and truth be told, they'd been fuller when we'd first met, but his large hand more than covered all of me. Yet, if there was even a millimeter he wasn't touching, I wanted him to find it.

His hand disappeared from between my legs at the same time he released my mouth and roughly pushed me to the bed. I went down easily, knowing what was next: Roman's order of operation.

First, he stripped my panties down my legs.

Second, he stripped his jeans down his legs and palmed his heavy cock as he stepped out of them.

Third, my personal favorite part, he dropped to his knees and sealed his hungry mouth over my clit.

A strangled cry escaped my lips, the pressure climbing high within me.

Fourth, one arm snaked up my chest, gripping my breast and sending the perfect balance of pain and pleasure searing through me.

And, lastly, when I was perilously close to falling over the edge, he thrust two fingers deep, coaxing the orgasm from the inside.

"Roman!" I moaned, fisting his hair as I rode my release out against his mouth.

When I stopped pulsing around his fingers, he lifted his head and rose to his feet.

"Back up," he ordered, prowling toward me, his hand glistening with my release as it pumped his cock.

Still in a post-orgasm high, I sluggishly shimmied up the bed, dropping my legs open as he followed me up on his knees.

Using my thighs, he stopped my ascent and dragged me back toward him. "Far enough."

"Condom," I breathed as he hovered over me.

His response was fast and final. "No."

"But—" I started.

He cut me off. "I'm not using a fucking condom with my wife."

"I'm not—"

"I swear to God, Elisabeth. Do not fucking finish that sentence."

And then the most incredible thing happened.

For the first time since Roman Leblanc had come back into my life, *I* didn't argue.

"I'm clean," I whispered.

"I know you are, baby, and so am I, okay?" he said, positioning himself at my opening.

"Okay." My eyes fluttered closed with anticipation.

And then he drove in with a gentle dominance that spurred orgasm number two to mercilessly rear up. The feeling of finally being full again overwhelmed me. My body shook as I fought a second release back. I wanted to ride it out with him, but emotions were scrambling my resolve, leaving me unable to hold back.

"Roman," I whispered, a single tear escaping the corner of my eye.

All at once, his arms slid under me and lifted me so he was on his knees, our chests smashed together, and my face tucked into his neck. "Shhh. Stay with me."

I folded my legs around his back while he used his upper-body strength to lift me up and down, setting a relentless rhythm that would have us both finishing in seconds rather than minutes.

I finally lost the battle and came as he speared into me, his arms squeezing me painfully tight. His speed increased, and then he planted himself to the hilt, groaning, "Lis," as he emptied inside me.

I clung to his shoulders as he lowered me back down to the mattress, our connection remaining until he shifted to my side. He was still holding me, but the loss was staggering.

He gathered me in his arms, tucked my face back into his neck, and brushed the hair off my neck.

We sat in silence for somewhere between a second and a century, his fingers lazily drawing patterns on my shoulder, before I finally found the courage to confess, "I miss you."

He sighed. "You have no idea."

My heart wrenched, and I couldn't keep the ache from my voice as I asked, "What happened to us?"

His arms spasmed around me, and then he kissed me hard on the top of my head, letting it linger for so long that I wasn't sure he was going to reply.

But, when he finally did, I still wasn't ready for the answer.

"Do you remember the lamb gyro?"

I stopped breathing, and he must have taken that as confirmation.

"Well, this time, I really fucked up. I actually lost you, and now, I'm lying here, praying that you'll let me fix it. Otherwise, I'm gonna look like a real ass when I propose tomorrow night and you say no."

A sound registering between a laugh and a sob came out, and I hugged him tight. "Please don't."

"I won't," he promised. "But you have to understand I will eventually."

"Roman," I pleaded.

"I can fix this," he declared.

"Stop."

"I can fix *us*," he swore.

"Please, stop."

"I *can* fix us."

"Hush." I kissed his chest.

"I *will* fix us, Elisabeth," he vowed. "Mark my words. I will not spend my life without you."

How do you argue with that?

"Okay," I agreed, completely unconvinced.

The sun had barely set when his body slacked under my cheek. "Okay," he repeated.

Minutes later, Roman fell asleep.

I listened to his breathing even out until I eventually followed him into dreamland.

And, in my dreamland, he was always there.

Even when he wasn't.

CHAPTER FIFTEEN

ROMAN

I woke up alone, just as I had every morning since she'd left. The hollow ache in my chest was my only company. I rolled to the side to check my alarm clock, and then my mind finally woke, too.

I was at home.

And not the piece-of-shit garage apartment I'd rented from an elderly couple when we'd first split.

I was *home*.

The room was dark, but the clock on her nightstand read only nine p.m. I couldn't have been asleep for more than an hour or two.

The day came back in a rush.

Heath Light

Walter Noir.

Clare.

Dread soured my gut.

And then…

Elisabeth.

Elisabeth.

Elisabeth.

My cock stirred to life as a smile split my mouth.

I scrubbed my hands over my face and pushed myself from the bed. The light in the bathroom was off, so I knew she had to be downstairs.

I dragged my jeans on, leaving my shirt discarded on the bedroom floor, then set about finding her.

The stairs of the old house creaked as I quietly made my way down. I froze in the middle when I heard her whispering in the kitchen.

"Because I'm freaking the fuck out!" she said quietly.

I could see her lower body pacing around the kitchen, the hem of a blue, silk nightgown brushing the tops of her thighs. It didn't appear that anyone else was in the house, so she had to have been on the phone.

I sank down to my ass and stayed out of sight. It was a familiar position for me. I'd done it numerous times in the six months after we'd lost Tripp. But, back then, it wasn't out of curiosity; it was out of desperation. I spent hours sitting on that step, listening to her laugh on the phone with one of her friends. She didn't laugh anymore back then—at least, not with me. I knew that, as soon as I hit the bottom step, she'd hang up and fall back into the pits of despair.

She needed the laughs. And my soul needed to hear her have them.

So, every Saturday morning before I darted off to work in an effort to create a way that I hoped would buy her smile back, I fed like a leech on the soft giggles that were no longer mine. And, when she'd finally hang up, I'd draw in a breath, walk the rest of the way down, and watch her smile slide away.

And then, like the coward I'd been, I'd leave.

Today would be different.

Tomorrow would be different.

Forever would be different.

She could fight me all she wanted. She could vent and freak the fuck out to whoever she was on the phone with. But, when I hit the bottom stair, I would *not* be leaving.

Ever.

I'd lived that life for two years, and I was done with it.

"He said he's checking back in. What does that even mean?" she whispered. "He doesn't just get to waltz back into my life and decide he's ready to start over. I'm pretty sure I get a say in this, too." She paused. "Oh, shut up! Sex is sex. It's totally different."

I bit my knuckle to stifle my laugh.

"He's an attractive man. I'm a woman with needs. And let's be honest—his cock is huge." I heard her giggle. "Then, if you don't want to hear about it, Kristen, don't bring up sex in the first place."

Dear Lord, it was Kristen. The good news was I knew she'd have my back. The bad news was I was starving, the smell of meat cooking was wafting up the stairs, and a conversation between those two could easily last all night.

Standing, I made my decision and then jogged down the last few stairs.

She was facing me with terrified eyes as I rounded the

banister.

"Hey," I said, raking a hand through my hair to get it out of my face, throwing an ab curl and a bicep flex in for good measure.

Clutching the phone at her ear, she stared at my chest and bit her bottom lip.

When I smirked, I swear to God the woman squeaked.

"Kristen, I have to go." She didn't say goodbye before hanging up.

My smile grew.

"Hey," she said, dropping the phone to the counter. Her eyes once again flashed down to my chest. "Do you…uh… need to borrow a T-shirt?"

I shook my head. "Nah. I've got clothes in my bag."

"Right," she said stiffly. Giving me her back, she turned toward the oven. "I…um…don't have an assistant to call for dinner delivery, so I made some burgers. You hungry? They're still warm. I was gonna come wake you up in a minute." She pulled a cookie sheet out of the oven and placed it on top of the stove.

Half of the pan was covered with my favorite seasoned sweet potato fries, and the other side had two handmade beef patties.

I snagged a fry, popped it in my mouth, then spoke around it. "Was this before or after you told Kristen about my huge cock?"

Her back shot ramrod straight. "I…don't know what you're talking about."

Chuckling, I slid a hand around to her stomach from behind and placed a kiss at the curve of her neck. "Fine. But you wanna tell me why you're freaking the fuck out?"

She sighed, her chin falling to her chest, her hand lifting to cover mine. "Oh, I don't know. Maybe because you're half naked in my kitchen right now after we had mind-blowing sex and where I confessed I miss you and you swore you were going to eventually propose again?"

"Mmm." I hooked my arm over her chest and pulled her flush against my front. "Yeah, but I said I missed you, too. And that I was gonna fix us. And then you made me burgers in a little, blue nightgown."

"I'm serious, Roman. This is too much. Combined with the embryo thing, I can't handle this right now. We need to slow down."

I inhaled deeply, filling my lungs with her sweet, floral scent, then kissed the other side of her neck. "How long did I wait the first time?"

She tried to step out of my grasp as she huffed, "This isn't the first time anymore."

"No. But, baby, you have to understand—we're creeping on two days since I got you back. This *is* me taking it slow."

"Roman, please. You can't fix years' worth of problems in minutes. I need time."

But she'd had two fucking years of time. I wasn't waiting even a minute longer. My life was with her. It always had been. It always would be.

I released her long enough to step in front of her. Then I shoved my hands under her arms and lifted her to sit on the counter beside the stove. Parting her legs, I stepped between them, resting my hands on her bare thighs and announced, "Shit went down today. And I really need to fill you in, but

I need your head straight on where *we* are before *we* can move forward to that."

"What went down today?" she asked, worry flashing over her face.

"Your head straight on what's happening between us yet?"

She scoffed. "No. But at least I'd know what shit went down today and won't be lost on both accounts."

I bent at the knees so we were eye level and said, "Let's get you straight. *Then* we'll talk about the shit."

She rolled her eyes. "Money has made you bossy."

"No. Living without you has made me realize that time's wasting. And I'm done watching the clock."

She opened her mouth to reply, but I silenced her with a kiss.

Her mouth was stiff at first, but it was Elisabeth. She soon became pliable.

And then she came alive.

Her arms wrapped around my neck, bringing me closer. I forced myself away when I felt the tip of her tongue touch my bottom lip.

I had minutes.

Not years—which is what it was going to take if her tongue entered the equation.

"I got out of the military because it wasn't ever going to provide me with the life I wanted for myself. I was a single, twenty-seven-year-old guy, and I wasn't getting any younger. When my time came up, the decision was easy. Between deployments, I had saved up around a hundred grand, so I moved home and dropped it all in a little building in downtown Atlanta in order to open Leblanc Consulting. I made twenty-two thousand dollars that first year. It was a fucking joke. But I had no doubt it could have been a success with time."

She raised an eyebrow. "I know all of this, Roman."

And she did.

But she didn't know the whys of my decisions back then—the same whys that had led me to make the decisions that had ultimately ruined us.

"When I met you, my entire world changed in one night. You were the best thing that had ever happened to me. But Leblanc Consulting wasn't going to enable me to give you everything I wanted to. I literally went from the bachelor life to a family man over night. You needed insurance, food, a house, and clothes. So I sold the building, took that entry-level corporate job in the city, put down a chunk of money on this house, finally bought you a diamond a quarter the size of the one I wanted, and then I made a life with you."

Betrayal sparkled in her deep-green eyes. "You told me you wanted that job in the city. You told me Leblanc Consulting was failing and you *needed* an out."

"I *needed* you to be happy."

"What?" Her voice broke as though I'd maimed her.

I quickly assured, "And I have never once regretted that decision. Because part of me giving you those things that made you happy made *me* happy. Watching you fall asleep with a smile on your face in a life I made for us was the most gratifying thing I'd ever done."

She stared at me in disbelief, her head shaking as she

said, "Roman, I wasn't falling asleep with a smile on my face because of the life you made for us. I was falling asleep with a smile on my face because I was doing it next to *you*."

"Right. And I got that even back then, baby. But, for a man, it's different. I can't expect you to understand, but I'm asking you to accept it. For a man, success is measured by your ability to provide a good life for your family. It doesn't have to be money, just a quality of life where your wife can fall asleep with a smile and doing it saying she's happy just to be doing it with you."

I thought she understood what I was saying when she stared at me for several beats without a response.

This was Elisabeth though.

I should have known better.

"Yeah. That makes no sense," she said. "This is why men get a bad rap. Y'all do stupid shit then try to justify it by saying crap like, 'For a man, it's different.' Sorry to be the one to break it to you, but if a man is kind, loving, respectful, makes a woman laugh, knows how to open the pickle jar, and change a flat tire, we really don't need much else. If I needed insurance, food, a house, or clothes, I would get off my ass, get a job, and get that stuff myself. What I can't get on my own is a good, kind, loving, respectful man who makes me laugh, knows how to open a pickle jar, and change a flat tire." She glared at me with an arched eyebrow.

I grinned and added. "With a huge cock."

She shrugged. "Doesn't hurt. But I could still make do if you didn't."

I threw my head back and laughed. God, I'd missed her. Her fingers traced over my abs as she giggled right along with me.

When I finally sobered, I pressed a closed-mouth, but no less deep, kiss to her smart-ass mouth. Then I got serious again.

I didn't want to do it.

What I really wanted to do was take a shower, drink a fucking beer, eat a homemade burger that was currently getting cold, then go to bed and make love to my wife before she fell asleep with a smile on her face, content to be doing it next to *me*.

But, again…I had minutes.

And years to make up for.

Palming each side of her face, I tipped my forehead to hers and got to it. "Lis, I spent my whole life thinking that, if you wanted something, you work hard and make it happen. And then, one day, I had to face the harsh reality that some things were out of my reach no matter how hard I tried. I couldn't give you a family, and it was the first time I ever felt like I'd failed you."

"Roman," she gasped, but I kept talking.

"It was a such a basic biological function, and I just couldn't do it. Do you have any idea how hard it was as a man to, month after month, watch the woman you wanted to give the world fall apart over pregnancy tests that just wouldn't turn positive? And then the miscarriages." I cleared my throat when a thick, gritty knot took up root.

"Roman," she breathed regretfully. "We both—"

"No, let me say this. It's been too long."

Tears welled in her eyes, but she closed her mouth and gave me a short nod.

I sucked in a breath and let five years of pent-up anxiety fly. "That fucking roller coaster of euphoria when you finally got pregnant, the constant nerves during those first few weeks, then the crash down into utter devastation when you'd start bleeding. Jesus, Lis. It destroyed me. I know it killed you too, but you were stronger than I was. You always got back up and wanted to try again. You have no idea how many times I wanted to tell you no. I couldn't handle it. I wanted it to stop so we could just go back to being us—being happy. But then I'd see that glimmer of hope in your eyes. So I'd pull my shit together and set about giving you the world, regardless that it was shredding me."

"Why didn't you say anything?" she accused, leaning away from me.

I was breaking her. I could see it in her eyes. Everything I'd shielded her from during those years we were trying to conceive was crushing her all over again.

I gave her space and swayed my torso back, but I kept my hips between her legs. "Because, if you wanted it, I wanted to be the one to give it to you."

She chewed on the inside of her cheek, tears streaming from her eyes. "I…I thought we were a team."

"We were!" I swore. "But, baby, infertility is an impossible sport. Everyone loses."

"Until they win," she replied sharply. "You're standing here, talking about our struggle to get pregnant and how that affected you. But you seem to forget the fact that we beat it. We got Tripp."

My eyebrows pinched together. I didn't know how to reply. I'd loved that little boy from the moment Elisabeth had told me she was pregnant. I'd never forget the first time I'd felt him kick. It was the first time I believed in miracles. I'd also never forget the day we found out he was a boy—and then, minutes later, found out about the fluid on his brain and that he probably wouldn't make it to delivery. It'd felt like I'd been hit by freight train. I wasn't sure we could consider that kind of tragedy a victory.

She closed her eyes and whispered, "You never connected with him, but I never thought you'd turn your back on me."

"I never connected with him?" I repeated on a violent whisper. "Have you lost your fucking mind? He died in my arms!"

"And then you left!" she yelled, pushing me back and hopping off the counter. "Like it meant nothing. Like those twelve minutes he was alive weren't worth it. You woke up the next morning while I was still in the hospital, grieving our little boy, and declared you were quitting your job and starting Leblanc Industries."

"So I could give you another child!" I roared.

Her face turned red as she screamed, "I didn't need another child! I needed *you*!" She began pacing the length of the granite island. "God, Roman. What is wrong with you? You act like I was some baby-crazed woman who wouldn't stop until I got a basketball team. I had just lost our son. The last thing on my mind was replacing him."

I stepped toward her, blocking her path. "But you would have wanted to try again eventually, Lis. And nothing had changed. I wouldn't have been able to give it to you. I couldn't do it physically, and it destroyed me when we had to borrow money from your parents the first time. That was my job to provide that for you. And I just couldn't! I started the company, and I did everything I fucking could to earn the money to pay for another IVF cycle." I pinched the bridge of my nose and stared at the floor. "I fucked up. I fucked up. I *fucked* up. I know this now. I should have talked to you. But, in the throes of failing the only woman I've ever loved, the words didn't come easily. I take full responsibility for that."

"God, Roman! You have no idea how often I used to lie awake in that bed, all hours of the night, just praying you'd come home and talk to me."

I slowly lifted my gaze to hers and admitted, "Yeah, I do. Because I used to sit in my car, down the street, waiting for your bedroom light to go off."

"What?" she whispered, a sob catching in her throat.

I reached for her hand, but she snatched it away.

"I couldn't stand watching you cry anymore and I couldn't fix it. I came home a few times and found you talking to my mom or one of your girlfriends, and for those moments, you were okay. Happy, even. But, as soon as your eyes met mine, they filled with tears. I figured staying away was better."

She shoved me as hard as she could. "You dumbass. I missed you. I missed our life. I missed being your wife. That's why I'd cry, because even when you did come home, you *still* weren't there!"

I lifted my hands palm up and, at a loss for more words, said, "I'm sorry."

"You're sorry? You're sorry? That's it?"

Was that it?

Not even fucking close.

I strode toward her, but she backed away just as quickly.

"Don't you dare come near me," she said. "Keep your hands to yourself and out of my hair so I can actually think for once."

This was not how this conversation was supposed to go.

"Lis, stop. Please. Let's just take a deep breath."

But she was far from done. "And I'm sorry, but I'm calling bullshit on your little give-me-another-baby excuse when it comes to your company. You signed over our entire life in the divorce in exchange for my half of your company." She marched forward and stabbed a finger in my direction. "Half that I never wanted! I fucking hate that company. I swear to God it's like the other woman in our relationship. I don't want your fucking money." Another step toward me. "I don't want any-fucking-thing that comes from that company or your precious little Rubicon." Her chest heaved when she finished. She kept her gaze locked on me as she glared expectantly.

Oh, I had a response. But she wasn't going to like it any more than I was going to like telling it.

"Three hundred and seventy-two"—I paused, bending at the waist before finishing—"*thousand dollars.*"

"What?"

"That's how much debt Leblanc Industries was in the day our divorce was finalized."

She gaped and repeated, "What?"

"You think I was eager to saddle you with half of that debt? Fuck that! I had nothing, Lis. But the woman I loved walked away with a house. Furniture to sit on. A bed to sleep in. A piece-of-shit car, but at least she had wheels. It wasn't much. But it was all I could give you."

Her face contorted murderously as she yelled, "Stop being such a goddamn martyr!"

I closed the distance between us in one long stride, catching her just as she crumbled.

Crawling even closer into my chest, she cried, "I hate you so much."

"I know," I breathed, kissing her temple.

"I spent two years of my life without you because you couldn't figure out how to open your fucking mouth and talk to me."

I hugged her as though I could absorb her pain. "I know. But I'm talking now."

"I don't wanna talk now." She whined. "I wanted to talk two years ago. I wanted you to stop me before I ever got to the door."

"I know. And I'm sorry." I kissed every inch of her face and hair that I could reach, her body shaking in my arms, the tiny remnant of my heart shattering all over again.

CHAPTER SIXTEEN

ELISABETH

My chest was tight, the ache lingering. I'd always been confused by the way our marriage had ended. However, hearing Roman's side of it definitely took some of the sting out. Even if I still couldn't completely wrap my mind around it.

I didn't know what all of it meant for us—as far as a future went.

To use Roman's words, my head was definitely not "straight" about what was happening with us.

But I knew with my whole heart that Roman still loved me.

And I knew with my entire being that I'd always loved him.

He was a bossy, suit-wearing, Range-Rover-driving, rich guy I barely recognized. But beneath it all was still my smart, funny, and gentle husband. So I didn't fight as he picked me up off my feet and carried me up the stairs to our bedroom, whispering a million apologies into my hair as we went.

He was still in jeans as he settled us both on the bed, and he wasted no time curling me into his chest. He combed his fingers through my hair until I relaxed on top of him. As I listened to the steady beat of his heart pounding out my favorite lullaby, my tears eventually stopped.

Then, in a bed we had bought together.

A bed where we'd spent countless nights laughing and talking about our days.

A bed where he'd made love to me with his hands, his mouth, and his body.

A bed where our children had been conceived.

A bed where he'd held me after we'd lost them.

A bed where he'd brought me breakfast and flowers every single Mother's Day.

A bed I'd fought the urge to burn on a near daily basis after we'd divorced.

A bed I realized I never wanted him to leave.

I finally got my head straight.

As I lifted my eyes, he looked down to meet my gaze.

"So, um…I guess you can keep the house key. Even though you stole it."

He grinned, and it lit his entire face, his perfect lips to his mischievous eyes.

I tipped my chin up, silently asking for a kiss—an offer he did *not* decline.

It was short but no less meaningful, and it caused a peace I hadn't felt in years to wash over me.

But a tinge of worry still lingered in the back of my mind.

"This isn't over. You know that, right? It's gonna take time to rebuild," I informed him just before he kissed me again.

With our lips still connected, he rolled us so we were on our sides, sharing a pillow. "Patience isn't my strong suit, Lis," he grunted, sliding a hand over my ass.

"Then you're gonna have to figure it out, because things happened, and they cut us both deep. It's gonna take time to heal." I brushed the hair off his forehead. "Now, I'm all for trying to do that healing together, but in order to do that, you're gonna have to find the strength to keep whatever twenty-pound diamond you've probably already bought tucked in your pocket."

This got me another blinding, full-face grin.

I leaned in to kiss his smiling mouth, but by the time I got there, it was no longer smiling.

It was open and sealing over mine.

He swallowed my moan when his tongue glided against mine. Then he fed me a groan as I threw a leg over his hips and ground against his cock.

Lifting my nightie, he shoved his hand inside the back of my panties, gripping hard and rocking me against him.

I lost his mouth as he knifed up, stripped the silk over my head, and threw it across the room. I found his mouth again seconds later as it landed on my breast, sucking my nipple deep and swirling around it with his tongue.

When I arched off the bed, he shoved an arm under my back, lifting me closer to his mouth.

"Oh God, Roman," I cried, writhing beneath him.

He shifted his attention to my other breast, setting off an explosion that traveled to my clit. My legs scissored beneath his heavy weight, but he was too lost in his feast on my chest to catch my silent plea for more.

His mouth was torturous. It took me high, but nowhere near high enough to fall. And, as he flicked his tongue over my peaked nipple, my body craved the release. I took the initiative and slid my fingers between my legs.

He growled and pushed up when he felt my hand move between us.

"Keep going," he demanded, rising off the bed, snatching my panties down my legs as he stood.

I dropped my knees to the sides, his eyes honing in on my fingers playing between my legs.

"Jesus, fuck, you're beautiful," he rumbled, dragging the tips of his fingers up my thigh, over my stomach, and then down the other side.

"Touch me," I begged.

Still staring down, he licked his lips then made the path up my other thigh, over, and down again.

"Haven't been with anyone else," he muttered.

"No one," I confirmed. "Touch me."

"Two fucking years and no one."

Up one thigh.

Down the other.

"No one," I repeated.

Up one thigh.

Down the other.

"I couldn't do it. I knew I'd get back here one day, and

I was not bringing another woman with me," he confessed.

My hand stilled as my mouth fell open.

He hadn't been talking about me.

He had been talking about himself.

Oh.

My.

God.

For the first few months after our divorce, I had become physically ill at the idea of Roman being with someone else. Then, after Rubicon had taken off, I'd accepted it as fact. On top of the sexy, smart, and charming man he'd always been, he'd become wildly successful and wealthy to boot. I'd figured women were probably lining up outside his office.

Now, hearing him say that he hadn't been able do it blanketed me in love.

"Keep going," he ordered, his hand still traveling up one thigh and down the other as he stood beside the bed, staring down at me.

My fingers went back to moving, but I was blinking tears back.

"No one?" I squeaked.

He finally lifted his eyes to mine. "I work a lot, but I could've made time. To date or whatever the hell people tell you to do after a divorce. But I always knew it wasn't over with us, and I refused to tarnish that with someone else."

Oh.

My.

God.

My throat closed, and that love flooding my system turned into an all-out wildfire.

Roman Leblanc was mine.

All of him.

Even when he wasn't.

Moving my hand to catch his wrist, I gave him a tug. "Come here, Roman."

He didn't move. He just continued to stare down at me, his face unreadable.

Swinging my legs over the edge of the bed, I sat up and kissed just above his navel.

Going for the button on his jeans, I told him, "I want to feel you, baby. Now's not the night for you to watch." I undid his zipper and pushed the denim down his legs, his thick erection springing free. "However, I'm gonna taste you first. So you can watch for a few minutes longer."

His abs rippled as I wrapped my palm around his cock and guided it to my lips.

"Fuck," he rumbled when I took him to the back of my throat.

I used my hand to work his shaft, my mouth paying special attention to his sensitive crown. His cock twitched with every swirl of my tongue. As I continued to slide him in and out of my mouth, one of his hands dipped to my breast, tugging on my nipple and shooting a tingle down my spine.

He brushed my long hair away from one side of my face, and I glanced up to find him watching, his gaze so intense that it caused goose bumps to pebble my skin.

"Missed your mouth, Lis," he said, fisting the back of my hair.

I cried out as he gave it a sharp, but still in-fucking-cred-ible, tug and popped himself free of my mouth.

"Missed watching you ride my cock more."

"Yes," I moaned.

I'd missed that, too. A hell of a lot.

He smirked. "You ready, baby, or you need me to help with that?"

If help meant his dexterous fingers finally finding their way inside me, then yes, I absolutely wanted help. But I didn't need it. I was more than wet and completely ready. And, judging by the glint in his smoky eyes, he wasn't just going to watch me ride him.

I knew that look well, and I was usually naked before he ever touched me whenever he wore it. He was going to take me from the bottom after he drove me to sheer insanity with his thumb at my clit.

It was *one* of his favorite ways to fuck me.

But it was my *absolute* favorite of all.

Because of this, I did not delay in standing, rolling up to my toes, ghosting my lips across his, and confirming, "I'm ready."

The side of his mouth hiked as he released the back of my hair and gave the bed a chin lift.

I followed his unspoken order and climbed up, watching him step out of his jeans and then prowl up after me.

He didn't touch me as he passed, but I shivered all the same as he settled his muscular body with his back to the headboard. My core clenched as he wrapped his large hand around his cock and gave it a firm stroke.

His gaze lifted to mine, his eyes so dark that they were barely recognizable. "Gotta say I love the way you're looking at me, but all I've had is my hand for the last few years. I'm gonna need you to get your ass over here, climb on top, and give me that pussy."

He did not have to tell me twice.

I moved at near pissed-off-Roman-Leblanc speeds (but not quite) and did exactly as he'd said. I climbed onto his lap, lined us up, and slowly sank down on his cock.

We both bit a curse back when I took him to the hilt. One of his hands went to my ass and rocked me back and forth as if he were trying to make sure I'd taken every last millimeter of him. It was not a hardship because my clit found much-needed friction on his stomach.

I closed my eyes, threw my head back, and ground down harder.

His hands found my breasts and began kneading and plucking as I glided up and down his length.

I set my pace and stuck with it even as his hands became frenzied.

"Find it, Lis," he growled.

I moaned an unintelligible response, leisurely enjoying the hunt.

Suddenly, his hips thrust up, slamming in deep and snatching my orgasm before I could even prepare.

"Roman," I cried, my body shaking as my release tore through me. My hands flew to his pecs for balance, but just as quickly, his arms folded around me, holding me still as he drove up inside me.

It wasn't his usual MO, but it was no less amazing. Thrust after thrust, his strong arms held me to his chest as he fucked me hard and fast. It was feral, and had it been any other man in the world, it would have been punishing.

But it was Roman, and he was back.

He was mine.

And I had always been his.

No one else.

I clung to his shoulders, biting and sucking up and down his neck as he bucked beneath me, slamming in deeper.

It didn't take long before another orgasm started to build, my entire body going tense as it rose within me.

"You gonna give me another one?" he asked on a pant.

"Yes," I breathed.

"Then hurry up," he ordered, driving back in.

As though I had a choice.

And I *really* didn't have a choice as he bottomed out inside me and circled his hips in an overwhelming combination I couldn't fight.

With my face buried in his neck, I let go and came apart in his arms.

He held me tight, gliding in and out for a few more strokes before he let go, too.

"Fuck, Lis," he hissed, his cock jerking as he emptied inside me.

I'd had sex with Roman more times than I could count, but never once had I felt like I'd lost a piece of myself in the process.

I was scared he couldn't say the same, because as I collapsed on his chest, his arms slack at his side, I knew with an absolute certainty I'd taken a piece of Roman Leblanc, and it filled me in immeasurable ways.

Something had broken between us.

But, in the process, something had also been repaired.

CHAPTER SEVENTEEN

ROMAN

Never in all of our years together had I taken Elisabeth so savagely. With the exception of having her hair pulled, she was a slow-build kind of girl. But it had been too long without her—I couldn't keep myself in check. She didn't complain though, and as her body sagged on my chest, sated and spent, I didn't figure she was going to.

"You good?" I asked the top of her hair.

"Mmmm," was her only reply.

I chuckled. "You gonna get cleaned up?"

"Can I say no?" she mumbled.

"You could. But you know you'll get up in the middle of the night and do it anyway."

She groaned but didn't move a muscle.

I gave her ass a squeeze and urged, "Come on, baby. I'll go down and lock up and get Loretta in. Meet you back here in a minute."

"You know, you never got your shower. Or beer. Or burger."

I smiled and gave her ass another squeeze. "No, but I got my fill of you. I'll survive."

She giggled, rolling off me.

I rose from the bed and went to my bag in the corner. My entire life was in that bag. I'd given Seth strict instructions about what to pack. All the clothes from my dressers—and my laundry hamper—sneakers, boots, and flip-flops from the closet, the gun from my nightstand, and a single picture of Elisabeth and Tripp taken minutes before he had taken his last breath. They were the only things I wanted from that shitty garage apartment. Sure, I had a closet full of suits and expensive shoes. There were also two computers, a big-screen TV, a ratty-ass couch, and about a million stacks of papers that had somehow migrated from the office over the years.

But I didn't care about any of that. I could lose everything else tomorrow, and as long as that bag sat in the corner of Elisabeth's bedroom, I'd have everything I'd ever need.

And, as I pulled a pair of boxer briefs on, looking at her as she sat naked and pink-cheeked on the bed while staring back at me, I decided I didn't even need the bag.

I walked back over to her and planted a fist on the bed. After a brief kiss, I said, "Clean up, baby. Two minutes. Want you right back here."

"Okay," she replied.

I kissed her again then headed for the door.

"Roman," she called.

I looked over my shoulder. "Yeah?"

"I'm sorry," she whispered.

My throat tightened. "Nothing—"

"For not seeing how deeply you were affected by the infertility stuff. For not understanding your reaction to losing Tripp. And, most of all, for not fighting harder for us."

"Lis…" I shook my head. "That is *not* on you."

"But it is. And I'm sorry."

I raked a hand through my hair and looked at her.

All innocent angel staring back at me.

My chest ached for the past even as my heart sped with possibilities of the future.

I opened my mouth to say…something. What, I didn't know.

It probably would have been, *I love you*, but I feared it would be, *Marry me.*

I would have meant both, but it was too soon for either.

She finally broke the moment with a soft, "Go get Loretta, baby. Two minutes."

I nodded but didn't move. I needed to say something. I wanted her to understand I didn't need an apology from her but I appreciated the fact that she had still given it to me.

"Two minutes," she repeated with a gentle and understanding smile.

I loved her so damn much that it physically pained me. I didn't want to wait to start our lives all over again. Elisabeth Keller had been born to be a Leblanc.

To be mine.

But, if she wanted to take this slow, I'd figure out a fucking way to make that happen—for her.

I tossed her a weak smile and finally got my feet moving.

After a brief standoff with the man in the hall mirror, I jogged down the stairs, let Loretta in, locked up, and then headed back up to spend the night with Elisabeth wrapped in my arms.

My wife.

The sound of the gunshot woke me from a deep content sleep. Elisabeth jerked on my chest, sucking in a deep breath in what I knew would become a scream. I slapped a hand over her mouth and rolled us both to the floor just as the second shot sounded outside the bedroom door. Loretta went nuts barking, and I heard feet scrambling down on the steps.

"Get in the fucking closet. Call nine-one-one. Do not come out until I come back to get you," I ordered.

Behind my hand, she wildly shook her head as her eyes bulged.

"Go. Now," I growled, releasing her and heading straight for my bag to retrieve my gun from the side pocket. "Phone, Lis," I said, sliding it across the floor.

She caught it and then scooped the dog up and rushed to the closet.

I didn't move to the door until I heard her shut herself in and her panicked voice say, "Yes, I need to report a break-in. There were gunshots inside my house."

With my back to the wall, my gun held high and ready, I swung the bedroom door open. I listened for a moment, but the house was silent. Still cloaked in darkness, I reached a hand around the corner to flip the hall light on, readying for an attack as my eyes adjusted to the light. As the hall came into focus, the man in the mirror didn't greet me. A million tiny cracks formed shards still held together but shattered completely, webbing out from two holes.

It seemed the man in the mirror put up one hell of a fight against whoever had made his way up the stairs, probably with his gun held high and darkness masking his true identity.

Slowly, I made my way down the stairs and found the place empty, the back door standing wide open. It was completely intact, nothing broken, nothing splintered. Just. Open.

It had been less than a minute since I'd left Elisabeth upstairs, and the sounds of sirens were already screaming in the distance. In a city the size of Atlanta, that was a miracle the likes of Moses splitting the Red Sea.

A loud boom at the front door made me spin, my finger poised at the trigger.

The door busted open, and it was only a nanosecond of hesitation that saved his life.

We stared, our guns trained on each other, when Agent Light said, "Gun down, Leblanc."

"Son of a fuck," I ground out, slowly lowering my weapon.

He kept his up. "You okay?" he asked, scanning the house.

"Yeah, we're good. What the fuck are you doing here?"

He didn't reply as he rushed past me, clearing the house,

and shutting the back door. When he was finally content that we were alone, he tucked his gun into his shoulder holster and stormed toward me. "You dumb fuck!"

"Excuse me?" I asked, my shoulders rolling back in defense.

The sirens drew closer.

"What the fuck did I tell you? Do not go off half-cocked!" he yelled.

"Light," I started, not in the mood for whatever bullshit he was about to sling. Elisabeth was upstairs in a closet, scared out of her gourd. I did *not* have time for his shit.

"You could have gotten her killed!" he roared, stabbing a finger in my direction. "Clare. Tessa." He paused, his face contorting with fury. "Elisabeth! Goddammit, Roman, I told you Noir was not to be fucked with. So you haul your ass over to his *house* and engage his *wife*? Who, by the way, I will fucking add, if you ever lay a finger on again, I will slit your goddamn throat myself."

"What did you expect me to do after you show me a picture of my child and tell me that she's in the arms of an abusive criminal?"

The muscles in his jaw clicked as he seethed, "I expected you to keep your shit together! But no, I had to sit my ass in a fucking car, watching *your* house all night long to keep Noir from coming in here and snuffing you out."

I took a step toward him, bringing us nose-to-nose, and whispered, "This was one of Noir's guys?"

He barked a humorless laugh. "Fuck, Leblanc. You signed your death certificate by showing up at that man's house today. Putting your hands on *his* wife. Trying to take *his* family. I want you to imagine for a second some man showing up at your house and pulling that shit. You'd fucking kill them. Now, I want you to imagine a piece of shit like Noir, who's killed men for innocently sitting in the same room as his woman." He leaned in close, his eyes flashing malevolent as he whispered, "He's gonna extinguish your entire family."

"Fuck you!" I spat, bile rising in my throat.

He shook his head and backed away. "No. You fucked us both."

Another surge of adrenaline hit me, causing my vision to tunnel. I didn't give one fuck who this Noir guy was. I'd set fire to his world if he thought he was going to lay one fucking finger on Elisabeth.

"Put your hands up," came from the front door, uniformed officers flooding in.

Heath kept his attention on me, his back to the door. "You need to get her away from here. You won't be this lucky next time," he said, slowly lifting his hands in the air. "Remember. Never seen me in your life."

"Right," I mumbled.

He nodded then called out, "Agent Heath Light. DEA. The suspect escaped out the back door."

"Drop your weapons!" the uniforms yelled in a round of chaos.

"Right," I mumbled again, squatting to set my gun on the floor.

Heath pulled his from his holster and did the same before retrieving his badge from his pocket. Once the cops were satisfied with his identity, he took over, passing orders out then getting on his phone to bark out more.

I didn't waste a single second before sprinting back up the stairs to Elisabeth.

The closet door was thankfully still shut, and it was only that sight that finally made my heart slow.

"Lis," I murmured quietly. "It's okay, baby. You can come out."

The door nearly clocked me in the face as it burst open and she came flying out. She launched herself into my arms, her green eyes consumed by fear. "Are…are you okay?"

"I'm good," I assured, holding her tight.

Her body trembled in my arms, so I scooped her off her feet and carried her to the bed, sitting on the edge with her securely in my lap.

She was terrified, but she was putting up one hell of a fight. Her chin quivered, but not a single tear fell from her eyes.

"The police are here," I told her, then kissed her forehead.

"I was so scared," she replied.

I guided her face into my neck, struggling with the knowledge that I'd inadvertently caused all of this. "I know, but it's over now. And everyone's safe, okay?" Judging by what Heath had told me, it was a lie, but I'd make it the truth. Somehow. Someway.

"What the hell happened?" she mumbled against my skin.

This time, I only half lied. "I don't know. You think you can get it together enough to come down and talk to the cops?"

She nodded then hugged me tighter, not budging off my lap. "I just got you back. I can't…" She trailed off.

My gut twisted. It was a sentiment I shared. If anything had happened to her… Fuck that. I was not going down that road.

I glided a hand up the back of her neck and tilted her head to force her eyes to mine. "No one. And I mean *no one* will take you from me. Or me from you, okay? I swear on my life I'll make us safe."

Her eyes suddenly narrowed. "Make us safe? It was just a break-in, right?"

"We'll talk later," I said, shifting her off my lap. "I need to get dressed."

"What aren't you telling me?" she asked my back as I headed toward my bag to pull on jeans and a T-shirt over my boxer briefs.

I ignored her and said, "You need to get…" I stopped when I glanced back and saw her standing there in what could only be described as a church dress. White. Floral. Hideous. "That is a seriously ugly-ass dress." A smile tipped one side of my lips.

She glowered. "I was naked and hiding in my closet from a gun-wielding burglar while my husband took off after him. I pulled on the first thing my hand landed on."

My smile grew as I arched an eyebrow and asked, "Your husband?"

"Don't you dare try to change the subject. What aren't you telling me?" she snapped.

"Later," I said, tugging the tee over my head.

"Roman!"

178

I leveled her with a glare. "I don't have the energy to deal with your attitude right now. The cops are crawling all over the downstairs, and they're gonna be making their way up here soon. We can talk *later* because, right now, I need to get *my wife* down there so they can take her statement while I make some phone calls and get our shit sorted for the next couple of weeks."

"Couple of weeks?" she questioned incredulously while crossing her arms over her chest.

Fuck, she was cute.

Cute was yet another thing I did not have time to deal with at the moment.

I didn't say a word as I walked over, took her hand, and dragged her to the door.

She quickly gave up with her argument when we got into the hall and she took in the broken mirrors. "Oh God," she gasped, covering her mouth with a hand.

Looping an arm around her waist, I took some of her weight and led her down.

Just as we got to the base, I saw an irate Detective Rorke standing close to a completely unfazed Heath Light.

"And you just *happened* to be passing by the Leblancs' house tonight when you heard gunshots," Rorke accused.

"Yep," Heath replied curtly.

"Seems awful convenient, Light."

"Sure does, considering no one ended up dead." He lifted his head when he saw us come down. His eyes landed on Elisabeth and stayed there as something eerie sifted across his features. "Excuse me," he told Rorke, already on the move in our direction. He stopped in front of Elisabeth, his eyes so intently studying her face that it unnerved me.

She must have felt the same, because she lifted a hand to rest on my stomach and shifted deeper into my side. "Um, hi?"

"Agent Heath Light, DEA," he said robotically.

"Elisabeth Keller."

"Leblanc," I corrected, then snapped my fingers at Light. His gaze slowly cut to mine.

I stepped around Elisabeth and tucked her into my back. Lowering my voice, I said, "I need the number of your security guy again."

He nodded, digging into his back pocket and pulling a card out while mumbling, "Finally, he does something smart." He passed the card my way. "Shoot me a text when you get free of this shit, and I'll forward you all of his info. He's in Chicago, but drop my name and he should be able to get some guys down here tomorrow. Get someplace safe until then. Yeah?"

"Yeah," I agreed immediately.

Elisabeth's hand tensed at my back, and I swung an arm back to pat her side.

It wasn't much, but in that moment, I had nothing else to offer her.

It was a common trend in our relationship.

But it was one I was planning to break.

I could fix this.

I would fix this.

I will fix this.

CHAPTER EIGHTEEN

CLARE

I woke up the next morning feeling run down and achy. I'd cried myself sick over the last few days.

When Walt had finally gotten to me the day before, I'd collapsed onto the driveway as I'd watched Roman speed away.

Walt held me, making my skin crawl as I protectively wrapped myself around Tessa. Both of us sobbing.

She was scared, and I couldn't blame her.

I was terrified, too.

Walt led us both inside and got us settled on the couch. Then he immediately retreated to his office. Over the next hour, a steady stream of his men came through the front gates, flooding in the back door, and going straight up to join him.

A man had come to help me. And I'd thrown him to the wolves.

And, as I sat on my couch the next day, Walt walking around in nothing more than a pair of slacks, not a trace of anger on his hideous face, I knew that that man was now dead.

I'd seen that picture Roman had thrust in my face. He had a wife, probably a child, and if his assumptions were correct and our embryos had been switched, it was *my* child. And I'd all but pulled the trigger myself.

The father of my daughter was dead.

But it was the wrong man. It was the kind and decent one who'd put his life on the line to save me—and Tessa.

And I'd killed him.

A tear escaped my eye, and I quickly swiped it away for fear of Walt noticing. I had a million reasons to blame it on after the last few days of drama, but I was all out of lies.

I couldn't help Roman anymore, but there was one man I could still save. I'd selfishly told Luke everything, putting his life at risk to make myself feel a moment of relief. I needed to stop him from repeating any of it before he was gone, too.

"I'm going to the gym this afternoon. I'll figure out dinner when I get home," I said as Walt started up the stairs to his office.

He stilled, one foot on the bottom stair. "I don't want you going back to that gym."

My heart leapt into my throat. "What... Why?"

"Why?" he asked incredulously, changing direction and heading back to me.

I steeled myself for an explosion and glanced to the kitchen, where Tessa was sitting at the table, playing with a giant ball of Play-Doh.

I stayed silent as Walt approached.

His knee landed beside me on the couch. The smell of his cologne made vomit rise in my throat. His hand went to my throat, sliding up and tilting my head back so I was forced to look at him.

My gaze flashed back to Tessa as panic ricocheted inside me.

Then, much to my surprise, he bent, kissing me chastely before saying, "Because, after the last few days, I don't want you out of my sight. There are men out there who think they can put their hands on my wife and still wake up breathing. You gotta know, sweetheart, that that shit does not fly. You're a Noir."

And I hated it more than anything else in the world. Carrying his last name was a punishment worse than any he'd ever doled out with his fists.

He gave my throat a gentle squeeze and trailed his other fingers down my chest, between my breasts, and down my stomach before stopping just short of between my legs.

I fought off the dry heave and did my best to control my breathing.

Walt was like a bear in the woods. He wanted dominance, and he demanded that you gave it to him. But, if you showed him fear, it only fueled him. He fed off the power.

I knew this game well. He wasn't going to hurt me—at least, not right then. But he wanted me to remember that he could.

However, victims often became the smartest players in the game of survival.

Puckering my lips, I silently asked for another kiss. He gave it to me then smiled menacingly.

I lifted my hand and teased the bare flesh at his stomach. "I'm yours, Walt. They touch me, they touch you."

"They touch you, Clare, they *die*."

"I'm yours," I murmured.

His eyes heated, so I kept talking.

"No one would be stupid enough to challenge you again."

He licked his lips.

Raking my nails up his sides, I pushed further. "You're Walter Noir. And I'm your wife. I'm untouchable, and I dare them to try."

"Fuck," he breathed, dropping his forehead to mine.

"It's just the gym, honey. A couple of hours on a treadmill to get my mind off the last few days." I slid my hand over his shoulder and into the hairs at the nape of his neck and whispered, "Don't let them win."

He stared at me, his eyes becoming soft at the corners. His stiff body uncoiling under my affection.

"Please," I added for good measure.

He gave in on a huff. "One hour. And Brock drives you."

It wasn't ideal. But it was something. And I *needed* to get to Luke and make sure he kept his mouth shut about everything I'd unloaded on him. Both of our lives depended on it.

I faked a grin. "Okay."

His hand tightened at my throat. "You run into any trouble whatsoever, I'll be there in a blink."

"I know."

He closed his eyes and inhaled deeply, breathing an, "I love you," on his exhale.

I fucking hate you. "I love you, too."

———◦◦◦◦———

The ride to the gym that afternoon was a silent one.

Brock pulled up in front. Then he got out and opened the back door so I could get Tessa out of her seat. When I had her on my hip, he slammed the door and grunted, "One hour." He then pulled around to a parking spot with clear visibility of the front door.

At least he isn't coming in.

"Hey, Clare!" the front desk girl, whose name I could never remember, chirped.

"Hey," I said, glancing around her toward the row of offices. "Luke in the back?"

"Uh," she stalled. "Actually, Luke didn't show this morning, but don't worry. I called in—"

The world stopped spinning.

I interrupted her on a nearly desperate cry. "What do you mean he didn't show?"

Her eyebrows shot up in surprise. "I mean…he didn't show up this morning."

My hands began to shake, and I shifted Tessa onto my other hip in order to lean my elbow on the counter for balance. "Did you try calling him?" I snapped.

"I did," she replied cautiously, "but he didn't answer."

My mouth dried. "Has…" I cleared my throat when the emotion prevented me from finishing. "Has he ever done this before? The not showing up thing?"

She shook her head. "No. He's usually here early. Let's just say Maxine was not excited to be called into work this morning to cover for him. She closed up last night after a full day of back-to-back clients…"

She continued to talk, but my ears were ringing, which left me unable to focus.

Please, God, don't let this be happening.

"Can you try to call him again? It's an emergency. I need to talk to him," I choked out. *To make sure he isn't dead.*

She frowned, eyeing me warily, but picked the receiver up and started to dial. "Sure," she drawled.

Please pick up. Please, just let him pick up.

I never tore my eyes off her as she did her best to avoid my gaze.

After a few seconds, she shook her head and hung up. She offered me a tight smile.

Oh my God.

It was not a coincidence that, only days ago, he'd met Walter Noir and, now, he was missing.

Fear and guilt mingled in the acid that replaced the blood in my veins.

Walt's words from that morning flashed into my mind. *"There are men out there who think they can put their hands on my wife and still wake up breathing."*

Men.

Not man.

Not just Roman.

And not just because I'd felt threatened.

Luke.

Because he'd cared. Walt must have sensed it when he'd stormed into the office.

Oh my God. He's gone.

"Clare!" I heard yelled.

Then, all at once, the Earth dropped out of orbit, taking me with it.

My knees gave out. The darkness closed in. My life flashed on the backs of my lids. My last thoughts were of Tessa. My only instinct still in tact was to protect her. As I hit the floor with a crash, she landed squarely on top of me, secured in my arms—the only place she was ever safe.

I was vaguely aware of voices clamoring around me and then Brock storming in.

But all I could see was the blood of innocent men pooling around me.

CHAPTER NINETEEN

ROMAN

After the cops had come and gone, Elisabeth and I had packed a few bags and the dog and headed for a hotel. The sun was starting to rise by the time we arrived. And, though we were both exhausted, adrenaline having burned through whatever rest we'd gotten, sleep wasn't going to be found.

Before our bags were even on the floor, I was on the phone with Heath's contact, Leo James. Elisabeth was listening with her mouth hanging wide open as I filled him in on all things Walter and Clare Noir. I wasn't far into the story when she began to tremble. I wrapped her in my arms, her heart thundering so hard that I could feel it in my chest.

Leo did not delay in telling me that he and a group of his men were catching the first flight down to Atlanta. It made me feel marginally better, but judging by the terror on Elisabeth's face, she did not share the sentiment.

When I hung up, she was plastered to my front and staring up at me expectantly.

"It's okay. Just breathe," I told her.

"She looks like me?" she squeaked.

I smiled and brushed the hair off her neck. "She's yours, baby. No question about it." I took her face between my palms. "We have a daughter, Lis."

"Oh God," she whispered.

"It's okay," I repeated, kissing her forehead. "Now that we know who they are, things should be easier. We'll have our attorneys petition the courts. See about getting the DNA then ultimately custody—"

She jerked in my arms. "Excuse me?"

"It's going to be time consuming, but I'll stop at nothing, Lis."

"We aren't taking that baby from her," she announced, stepping out of my grasp.

This time, I jerked. "Come again?"

"Roman, we *aren't* snatching that child away from the only mother she's ever known. *Especially* if what Heath told you was true and Clare's a victim in all of this too."

"Yeah, baby. She's a victim, but I saw her. You cannot help someone who doesn't want to be saved."

"You probably just scared the shit out of her, Roman! Some man shows up at my house. Grabs me in front of my child. I wouldn't be real keen to jump in his car, either."

"Maybe. But I tried. And she screamed for the man who beats the shit out of her. That does not say scared to me. That says fucking *lost*."

She flinched. "We can't just storm in there and strip the

189

child from her arms. As a mother, I would never be able to live with that."

I released her and made my way over to the pile of shit we'd brought with us. I dug through it until I found what I was looking for then headed back to her.

Lifting Heath's picture of a battered Clare Noir in her direction, I said, "He does that to her." I dropped it to the floor then lifted another. "And that."

Her body turned to stone as she slapped a hand over her mouth.

"And our daughter lives under the same roof with that man, Lis. This whole fucking situation sucks. Hell, the fact that a man like that is sharing the same oxygen we breathe is fucked. But there is nothing I can do about that, either. I know this is hard for you to understand. You're a good person with a good heart. Your gut instinct is to save the world. And, usually, I'm right there with you. But you need to hear me on this. I have no control over Clare. The only thing I can do in this situation is keep my *family* safe." I lifted one final picture in her direction and finished, "That family now consists of you, me, and *this* little girl."

Her eyes flashed wide, and just as quickly, the picture of Tessa was snatched from my hand. She stumbled back until she hit the bed. Then she slowly sank down, her eyes glued to the photograph.

I sat beside her and slid an arm around her back. "Let me worry about her. I don't like the idea of snatching her away from the life she knows, either. But, Lis, that life is *dangerous*. I gotta tell you I'd be just as hell-bent on getting her out even if I wasn't sure she was ours. No kid deserves to grow up like that. But the fact is no one can deny that that little girl is yours. So I will fight like hell to get her someplace safe—that place being with *us*. And when, and only when, we make that happen, we'll see what we can do about Clare."

Her tear-filled eyes lifted to mine. She was looking at me, but I knew she was still seeing Tessa's face.

"Okay?" I prompted.

She nodded and looked back at the picture. Her fingers glided over the curves of the child's face. "Okay, Roman."

I breathed a relieved sigh and squeezed her shoulder. "Now, baby, I know you've had a lot dumped on you, but we gotta figure out where we're gonna live for a little while. I'm not taking you back to our house, and my place is shit."

"My Victorian," she whispered at the picture.

"Say again?"

"I own an old Victorian house. I flipped it. I've been trying to sell it, but it's currently empty. All the utilities are hooked up. And I'd feel safe there."

"It furnished?"

She shook her head.

"Right. Okay. I want a bed, couch, TV, some kind of table we can eat at, and whatever the hell else you need to feel comfortable." I dug my wallet from my back pocket and pulled my credit card out before offering it her way.

She glanced down at the card then up at me. "All of that's going to be expensive, Roman."

I grinned. "I think I'm good for it."

"We really don't need that much stuff. I've got an air mattress and a couple of chairs there already."

"An air mattress and a couple of chairs?" I repeated incredulously.

She bobbed her head eagerly. "We can make do."

No fucking way was Elisabeth ever *making do* again. I'd worked my ass off and even lost her for over two years to ensure that.

"Seven point four million dollars," I announced.

Her mouth fell open, and her eyebrows pinched together. "Holy shit. Is that how much you're worth?"

I chuckled and waved my credit card at her. "That's what I made last month. Buy some furniture, Lis."

She clamped her mouth shut and blinked, but a few seconds later, she took the card.

After a shower, which had been just as mentally cleansing as it had been physically, I got to work calling our attorneys. Kaplin was still unsure of our next move. However, Whit was hitting the ground running. He had Detective Rorke on the phone before he'd even hung up with me.

During this time, Lis alternated between staring at the picture of Tessa, petting Loretta, and scrolling through furniture on the Internet. She was lost in her thoughts—and her pain.

I never strayed far from her. Not for fear, but rather for comfort. If she needed me, I was mere feet away. I kissed her every chance I got. And, as I paced the room, trying to figure out the best solution for...well, anything, I'd paused to drag my fingertips over her shoulders, reminding her that she wasn't alone.

She'd glance up at me with a forced smile that broke me every time.

But I was there.

And she was with me.

We'd figure out the rest together.

Around two p.m., Leo James, along with three of his men—Aidan Johnson, Alex Pearson, and Devon Grant—arrived at the hotel. I was a big guy. But fuck, Alex and Devon were giants. And Johnson was just flat-out scary—tattoos running up and down both arms, black gauges in his ears, brute terror in his eyes.

"Leo, nice to meet you," I greeted, ushering them to the sitting area of the suite. "Gentlemen, this is my wife, Elisabeth Leblanc."

Her gaze jumped to mine, but she didn't argue with my use of my last name. I shot her a wink then continued with the introductions. When I finished, she smiled blankly and offered a soft, "Hi."

I settled beside her on the couch, hooking her legs at the knees and dragging them into my lap so they draped over my thigh.

She inched closer and dropped her head to my shoulder.

"Mrs. Leblanc," Leo said, settling in a chair across from us. "I hear you guys have been having some trouble recently?"

"I'm not sure *trouble* is the right word," she replied.

"Well, I'm here to help you two take care of that." He grinned warmly, leaning toward her, propping an elbow on his knee, and leveling his dark-brown eyes on hers. He lowered his voice and soothed, "I promise, Elisabeth, I've gone toe-to-toe with far bigger men than Walter Noir. I know what I'm doing here, so I need you to trust that me and my men are gonna keep you two safe. That way, you can focus your energy on getting your little girl out. Leave the rest to us. Can you do that?"

Her body relaxed for the first time all day, sinking deeper into my side.

Even if he did absolutely nothing else, this guy was officially worth every fucking penny of the six figures I'd already paid him.

"Yeah, Leo," she whispered.

He gave her a chin jerk then turned his attention back to me. "I don't have a ton of time here, Roman. Johnson and I have to head back to Chicago tomorrow. I'm leaving Alex and Devon for you to use at your disposal. Get them a schedule of places you need to go ahead of time, and they'll handle the logistics of the whens and hows to get you there safely. In the meantime, we need to discuss this house I understand you two will be staying at."

"The Victorian," Elisabeth added.

Leo looked back at her, grinned, then all but motherfucking purred, "Yeah, that one, babe."

Babe?

"James," I warned. My lips thinned, and I cocked my head to the side while shooting him a dangerous glare.

The corners of his twitched as he leaned back in his chair, holding my gaze while pointedly rotating a gold wedding band around his ring finger with his thumb. "Anyway, the Victorian," he said. "I'll need the keys. Johnson and I will be working with a security company to get it wired up before we leave. I want you guys to stay here tonight. You're gonna need to call down to the front desk. I want my guys in the room next door. If it's not available, you're gonna need to change rooms, hotels, or, fuck, cities if need be. But I want my boys in earshot in case anything goes down."

"I can do that," I replied.

At the same time, Elisabeth sat forward and gasped, "You think something else is going to go down?"

Every man in the room spoke at the same time. "No."

I pulled her back into my side and kissed her temple. "Baby, I swear you're safe."

She looked up at me, her eyes filled with fear, but when she opened her mouth, a familiar attitude came out. "I'm sorry, Mr. Lock Me In A Closet Then Run Out With A Gun Chasing The Man Who Broke Into Our House In The Middle Of The Night And Put Two Bullets In Our Wall. You'll have to excuse me. But it's not *me* I'm worried about here."

I scowled at her while I listened to the guys chuckle. "You worried I can't handle myself?"

Her lips formed a hard line as she adamantly shook her head. "No. I'm scared that *you* would not hesitate in getting yourself killed if it meant keeping *me* safe."

"Not even for a second," I confirmed curtly.

Her eyes narrowed, and her eyebrows pinched. "Then, *clearly*, you understand why I'm afraid here."

I twisted toward her, forcing her back against the couch with my upper body. "Nothing's going to happen to me, but if it does, you'll deal. But make no mistake about it, Lis— you will do it with a pulse."

"Roman!" she objected, shoving at my chest.

"Okay," Leo interrupted. "Let's calm down. This is just precautionary stuff at the house. But let's make a deal here. Elisabeth, your man, Mr. Lock You In A Closet Whatever The Fuck You Called Him, will make sure no one touches you. And Alex and Devon will make sure no one touches your man. Everyone's covered. Okay?"

After a second, she grumbled a quiet, "Deal." Glowering at me, she added, "But you should know—you pin me to a damn couch again, Roman, you are going to need men far bigger than those two to keep you safe."

This received a chorus of deep chuckles—one of them being mine.

I casually righted myself on the couch and gave Leo my attention. "So, what's next?"

He smiled and shook his head, glancing over at the three guys looming around us. "Get your rooms for the night settled. Assuming all goes well with the security system, I should be able to get you into the house before I leave tomorrow night."

"Elisabeth needs to go shopping for furniture," I informed.

Leo arched an eyebrow. "You going with her?"

I replied by stating, "She was looking at floral throw pillows earlier."

"Technically, they were damask," she corrected.

Leo glanced from me to her and then back again. "Right. Alex. Devon. Take the lady shopping. Roman, you're with Johnson and me at the Victorian."

I grinned.

Johnson laughed.

Alex and Devon mumbled curses.

Elisabeth giggled.

Leo grinned back.

Yeah. Worth. Every. Fucking. Penny.

CHAPTER TWENTY

CLARE

True to his word, Walt rushed to my side when he found out that I'd collapsed at the gym.

I'd cracked the back of my head on the floor, splitting it open, but despite the urging of the gym staff, I'd refused to go to the hospital and have it stitched up. I'd taken care of far worse injuries on my own, and going to the hospital meant leaving Tessa with Walt.

No. Fucking. Way.

I assured everyone that I was okay, and then, as Walt and Brock shared angry whispers at the door, I quietly asked the front desk girl to call me immediately if Luke happened to show up.

He wouldn't. But the only thing I could do was hold on to a shred of hope.

My head was aching as I strapped Tessa into her highchair for dinner.

She was chasing blueberries around her tray with two wooden spoons as I finished up the lasagna I'd insisted on cooking as a way to keep my mind off all things Roman and Luke.

It hadn't worked. If anything, it had given me entirely too much time to obsess as I mindlessly prepared dinner.

By the time the oven timer went off, my guilt had become poisonous, which was causing my hands to shake and my stomach to knot.

"Hey," Walt greeted, folding his arms around me from behind.

My body turned solid, and tears flooded my eyes.

"What's wrong, sweetheart?" he murmured, placing a kiss at my neck.

It was one of the many times in my life I should have kept my mouth shut. The first being the day Walter Noir had asked me out on our first date. The second being the day he'd slid his ring on my finger. But, just like in those instances, the words flew from my mouth before my mind could intervene.

"Did you kill that man who came to the gate yesterday?"

His head popped up and he squeezed me tightly. "So that's what's going on inside your head. You're worried about that piece of shit?"

I couldn't tell if he was pissed or concerned, so I stuttered, "I...I just—"

He turned me around and used my chin to force my gaze up to his.

I sucked in a sharp breath when I found his face soft, a comforting grin tipping one side of his mouth.

"Not yet," he whispered. "But I swear to you he will be taken care of *very* soon. You'll never have to deal with him again. No one touches you, remember?"

A shot of adrenaline jumpstarted my system.

Not yet.

Not yet.

Not. Yet.

A sob of relief tore from my throat, my body shaking in his arms.

Roman was still alive.

"Jesus," he breathed, tucking my face into his neck. "I had no idea you were this scared." He rubbed his hand up and down my back.

It was one of the only moments of solace I ever got. I hated him and wished he'd die on a daily basis, but I was so starved for comfort that I'd accept whatever I could get—even from him.

His gentleness made me momentarily forget the monster in disguise, and I asked, "What about Luke?"

His hands stilled, and I realized I'd made a huge mistake.

I could have been scared of Roman, but I had absolutely no reason to fear Luke. So my asking about him could only be construed as interest in Walt's warped mind.

"Luke? Your personal trainer?" he whispered maliciously.

My mind scrambled for a cover. "I…I was just trying to figure out if I needed to hire someone new. That's all," I said, attempting to move away.

But his once gentle hands turned punishing in the span

of a second.

I was still wrapped in his arms when he squeezed me painfully tight, my lungs protesting and my tender ribs screaming. "I…can't…breathe…" I choked.

He nuzzled his jaw against the side of my face and drawled, "Good."

I struggled in his arms, the combination of fear and his grip making it nearly impossible for me to breathe. I was on the verge of passing out again when he suddenly released me. He didn't move away as he watched me fight to draw air into my lungs. He hovered over me, a venomous glint in his eyes.

"Please," I begged, stumbling away, drawing him away from Tessa, knowing from experience what would follow.

I hadn't gotten far when he caught me, the tips of his fingers biting into the backs of my arms.

"He's dead," he sneered, rearing one of his hands back.

I closed my eyes preparing for the blow, but it never came.

I pried my eyes open, and he grinned, brushing the back of his hand down my cheek. A moan of approval rumbled in his chest when I flinched.

"I gutted him with my own hands," he said, trailing his fingers down my eyes, my nose, and then my chin. "You should have heard him screaming to God for help. Such a fucking coward, that one." He kept his eyes locked on me as he asked, "You don't have a problem with that, do you, sweetheart?"

I hid my wince and fought the vomit crawling up the back of my throat, keeping my shield firmly in place as I replied, "Not at all, honey."

It was the wrong thing to say.

But I'd learned with Walt that there was never a *right* thing to say.

"Not at all, honey?" he whispered, gripping my neck and lifting me to where I could barely keep my tiptoes on the floor. "Not at all, honey?" He laughed, dropping me back down. "Not at all, honey!" He yelled at the top of his lungs, spit flying from his mouth as a heavy hand struck my face.

I stumbled back as pain exploded within me.

Tessa screamed from her chair as Walt roared, "Liar!"

"I'm not lying about anything," I cried, my hand covering my swelling cheek.

"You fucked him. You whore!"

I adamantly shook my head. "I didn't! I swear. He never laid a finger on me."

He stormed forward, and I retreated as fast as I could, stopping only when my back hit a wall.

He slammed his palm on the wall beside my head and leaned in, snarling, "Trust me, he wanted to."

"No," I stated firmly.

He held my gaze and searched my eyes.

My heart raced, blood thundering in my ears, and I had to hold my breath to keep from exposing my fear, but I finally managed to repeat, "No."

Anger still radiating off him, he shoved off the wall and backed up a step. "Well, then I have some good news for you, Clare. As far as I know, Luke is alive and well." He cracked his neck. "For the next half hour, anyway. What's his last name?"

Any relief I'd had when I'd heard he was alive morphed into paralyzing fear. "Walt, no," I gasped, shaking my head.

"If this guy means nothing to you, give me his fucking last name."

Frantically trying to come up with a distraction, I stepped forward and rested my hands on his chest. "I swear to you he means nothing to me, Walt. But that doesn't mean he needs to die."

He swatted my hands away. "Name. Now. Or you *will* regret this."

But I already regretted everything. I couldn't add Luke's death to that—not again.

"Please don't do this," I pleaded, reaching out for him once more.

Suddenly, he turned on a toe, giving me his back as he headed toward Tessa.

My heart constricted as I flew after him. "Walt! Stop!"

"Mama!" she shrieked, fighting to get out of her seat as he approached.

I rushed around him, blocking him from advancing any farther.

I fully expected him to plow over me. But he came to a halt, his hand stabbing into his pocket to retrieve his phone. He quickly dialed a number and lifted it to his ear.

"His name, Clare. Right. Fucking. Now." He pointedly glanced over my shoulder at a now hysterical Tessa.

Walt had never gone after Tessa before, so I had no idea what he was trying to insinuate, but it was my daughter, so I wasn't about to wait to find out.

It was the exact moment my soul broke in two.

One part would forever be with Tessa, and the other would be buried in a shallow grave with a man whose only mistake was being kind.

"Cosgrove," I whispered, the pain searing through me.

He barked, "Luke Cosgrove," into the phone. Then he turned on a heel and strode out the front door, slamming it behind him.

Tears sprang from my eyes, and the heave of my stomach threatened to overtake me. I managed to get Tessa out of her chair and both of us locked in my bedroom and then locked in the bathroom before I lost it.

She crawled into my lap, curling as close as possible as I threw up in the toilet.

How is this my life?

I couldn't do it anymore, but I knew with a certainty I could feel in my bones that Walt would never let me go.

He was going to kill me one day.

The only thing I could do was make sure Tessa wasn't there to witness it.

It would gut me, and I'd live the rest of my short life soulless and empty, the promise of dying being my only reward.

But I now had it in my power to make sure she wouldn't suffer the same fate.

She was young; she'd forget me eventually.

I never would though.

At least, this way, I could let go and allow death to swallow me with the vision of her smiling branded on the backs of my eyelids.

Sobbing, I rose to my feet with her snuggled in my

arms. "Mama's gonna take care of this, baby," I whispered, carrying her to my bed. "You're gonna be okay."

I climbed into bed, held her impossibly tight, and cried myself to sleep, mourning the loss of my only child.

CHAPTER TWENTY-ONE

ELISABETH

Ten days later...

"Calm down," Roman urged.

"Oh God. Oh God. Oh God."

"Elisabeth," he called, shaking my shoulders.

I clung to his shirt, fighting for breath, as an all-out panic attack tore through me. It wasn't my finest hour. It was, however, thirty minutes before the entire Leblanc family was set to descend upon my old Victorian for Thanksgiving dinner and I had just burned the bottom of the sweet potatoes.

Roman and I had been taking it slow. Which, for us, meant we'd furnished an entire house together, he'd moved in, we'd taken two full weeks off work so we could spend every day together, he'd made love to me every night, and I'd fallen in love with him all over again. Not that I'd ever fallen out of love with him, but it was different this time.

Time had changed both of us.

But, dare I say, this version of Roman Leblanc was even better. He pissed me off with his bossiness, but it only made the moments when he was tender that much sweeter.

We had bodyguards watching us twenty-four-seven, but he never made me feel like I was trapped inside the house. He worried about me—I could see it in his eyes. But, if I wanted to go somewhere, I went. And, depending on the task, he sometimes came, too.

Not everything had changed though. We still laughed like maniacs, slow-danced in the shower, and occasionally ate dinner on a blanket on the dining room floor instead of at the table.

It wasn't all a walk in the park though. I was still struggling with the past and our new reality. Our attorneys were working around the clock, and we waited with bated breath for a judge to sign off on our request for DNA testing. It wasn't an easy sell, but with Rorke and his team working on their end, we had hope someone would come through for us.

Tessa weighed heavily on our minds. I prayed that she was safe. And, if I was being honest, I prayed the same for Clare. I couldn't imagine what she was living through, but Roman was right. Our first responsibility had to be Tessa, but that didn't mean I'd give Clare up.

I'd framed the grainy surveillance photo of Tessa and placed it on the nightstand next to a picture of Tripp. Then I promptly lost it when I realized, if Tessa was ours, it probably meant that Tripp wasn't.

Roman held me until I was out of tears and eventually fell asleep in his arms. The next morning, I awoke and found him fully dressed, sitting in bed, holding a scrapbook that I knew had still been in my nightstand at the old house.

I'd started it when we'd first decided to do IVF. In that book was everything from the beginning to the end: ultrasound follicle pictures from when I was in the stimulation phase. Pictures of Roman and me wearing those hair nets doctors wear in surgery—it was taken just minutes before they'd put me under for our egg retrieval. There was another picture of us in the exact same pose taken five days later as we held a tiny picture of two beautiful embryos while waited for them to be transferred back into my uterus.

Then the images changed. There was a picture of us holding a positive pregnancy test, both of our eyes filled with tears. It was followed with weekly belly pictures leading up to our twenty-week ultrasound, where we found out about Tripp's condition. But, even through my grief, I still documented every moment of our little boy's life.

On the last page was a picture of his tiny body snuggled into my chest, Roman's hand on his back, a huge smile on both of our faces. The name *Roman Daniel Leblanc, III "Tripp"* in huge letters at the bottom of the page.

Roman smiled as he placed the album in my lap then kissed my forehead. "Lis, he was ours in every way that mattered. He was created with love, born with love, and died with love. Not everyone can say that."

Oh, yes. I loved Roman Leblanc.

So, with tears in my eyes and a photo album of our baby clutched to my chest, I filled him in. "I love you."

He grinned, the twinkle of the man I'd first met all those years ago dancing in his silver eyes as he said, "I love you, too. I never stopped, and I never will."

That afternoon, we went to visit Tripp's grave together for the first time ever.

The peace I felt while standing in Roman's arms as we both spoke softly to our little man was indescribable. When we got home later that night, just before we fell asleep, Roman confessed that, the day I'd buried Tripp's ashes at the cemetery, he'd spent the afternoon in my empty house, sitting on the edge of our old bed, trying to figure out how that had become his life.

It broke my heart, but I held him tight and assured him that that life was over for both of us. And I meant it. I wasn't a fortune teller, but I still knew that Roman was here to stay. Mainly, because I flat-out refused to ever let him go again.

After that, he sat in bed, laughing, as I gave him a ration of shit because, if he had been sitting on my bed a year ago, he had clearly broken in.

We both fell asleep with smiles on our faces.

Content for no other reason than we were doing it together.

Which brings us back to the now. Thanksgiving Day. Burnt sweet potatoes. Me in an all-out panic about that— but mainly about spending a holiday with Roman's family for the first time in years.

"Chill out," he said, palming each side of my face and dipping his forehead to rest on mine.

"Oh God. Oh God. Oh God," I replied.

Then I chilled out because his hand slid into the back

of my hair and he tipped my head back so his mouth could cover mine.

I moaned as his other hand made it down to my ass.

He kissed me just long enough for me to forget my potatoes, but not his family. Therefore, when he released my mouth, I only said, "Oh God," once.

"Baby," he started. A man like Roman Leblanc did not roll his eyes, but right then, I could sense that he was fighting the urge. "I'll go to the store and buy some more fucking potatoes."

"It's Thanksgiving, Roman. Nowhere is going to be open."

"Then I'll find a fucking field and dig 'em up myself. Just calm the hell down, Lis."

"Screw the potatoes. Your family is coming over!" I gripped the front of his T-shirt.

Yeah, Roman was back to his old uniform. I hadn't seen him in a suit since that day at the police station. Albeit his old uniform had gotten a seriously pricey overhaul, but they were still jeans and T-shirts, so I could deal with it. My man was sexy all the time, but something about him in washed-out denim did it for me.

He eyed me skeptically. "That's usually what happens after you invite family over and then spend a week hashing out the details of who is bringing what."

I scowled as his lips twitched with humor. "I know this, *Roman*. But I haven't seen your family in years."

"You saw Kristen yesterday."

"Yes, but—"

"And I know you've seen my mom semi-recently. She

loves to rub that shit in my face every time she sees you."

"She rubs it in your face?"

He nodded. "Lis, I've been in love with you for years. Moms have a knack for reading between the bullshit. She loved you and made no secret of the fact that she wanted us back together. So yeah—every single time she saw you, I got a phone call the next day telling me how beautiful and happy you looked. And how you did whatever-the-fuck nice thing you happened to do while she was with you. And, because she's my mother, I couldn't even hang up on her."

I giggled. I loved Cathy Leblanc. And I loved that she loved me enough to punish her own son for being a dumbass. "Your mom is amazing."

He grinned. "So, basically, you're worried about my dad?"

"No. Rome has always loved me."

And he had. He hadn't batted an eye when he'd found out Roman and I were already married when he first met me, which was only approximately forty-eight hours after I'd met Roman. He'd just slapped his son on the back and congratulated him for recognizing a good woman when he'd found one. Simple as that.

"Okay, baby, I don't have any long-lost brothers you don't know about. Kristen, Mom, and Dad are the only ones coming over. And you've already admitted that you love them all. Care to let me in on what exactly you're flipping your shit about?"

"It's not just Kristen. Or Cathy. Or Rome. It's all of them. At the same time. And I don't even know what the current state of our relationship is."

His eyebrows furrowed together as he frowned. "Okay, now, we have a problem. What in the ever-loving hell do you mean you don't even know 'the current state of our relationship'?"

Yep. He totally tossed me a pair of air quotes.

I rolled my eyes. "I mean…how are we presenting this to them? Am I your ex-wife? Girlfriend? Wife?"

He stared at me blankly before grunting, "Yes."

"Yes. What?" I threw my hands out to the sides in frustration.

I was up off the floor before I knew it. My ass landed on the counter, Roman wedged between my legs, his hands on my hips.

"Was I inside you last night?"

He had been. And we both knew it.

"Jesus, Roman." I glanced around to make sure Devon and Alex weren't in earshot.

I guessed he took that as my answer, because he continued. "You love me?"

"Of course," I replied immediately.

"You planning to make a life with me?"

"I…I…" I stuttered in surprise.

He arched an eyebrow.

"I mean…yeah. I was kinda hoping to." I began chewing on my bottom lip.

We hadn't talked about the future yet. Though it was kind of a given.

He smiled and moved his hands to the counter, one on either side of me, and kissed me—hard.

My body responded immediately, my nipples tingling,

my toes curling, sparks igniting.

Ya know, the usual when it came to Roman.

I slid a hand around his neck and slanted my head to take it deeper. His tongue glided with mine as I shimmied to the edge of the counter and locked my legs around his hips.

He continued to kiss me, but I became vaguely aware of him digging something out of his back pocket.

My stomach fluttered in the best possible way.

Oh. God. This was it.

He was going to propose again.

I was actually impressed he'd made it nearly two weeks.

My heart pounded in my chest as I asked, "W-what are you doing?"

I felt something land on my thigh, both of his hands fumbling with it.

I pried my lips from his and glanced down to see his hands digging in his wallet.

Then out came a ring.

Only he slid it onto his own finger.

"Uh…" I dodged his lips as he attempted to catch my mouth again. "Did you just give yourself a ring?"

"No. I just put the ring you gave me back on," he said, moving in for another kiss, but I turned my head, so his lips landed on my cheek instead.

"You keep your wedding ring in your wallet?" I had no idea why *that* was the part that had surprised me most.

"I only took it off to get people at the office to stop asking questions. But you gave me that ring. I sure as fuck wasn't going to hide it away in some box at the top of my closet. Why? Where's yours?"

I bit my lip and looked away sheepishly. "In a box at the top of my closet."

Chuckling, he pressed his lips to my temple. "I'll send Devon to go get it. You need to at least be wearing your engagement ring when my parents get here. Considering I already told them we were getting remarried."

I swung my head to face him, my eyes bulging in disbelief. "You did not!"

He shrugged.

"You didn't even ask me yet. I have the right to refuse."

He twisted his lips and gave me a teasing side-eye. "You were gonna say yes."

"You don't know! I could totally say no."

This time, he laughed, throwing his head back and everything.

"Roman, I'm serious," I scolded.

Still laughing, he looked back at me and said, "I have no doubt that you are, Lissy. But I also know you would have said yes at the police station if I'd asked."

"I would not!"

"You would."

"I would not."

"You would."

"I would *not!*"

He leaned in close. "You *would.*"

"Roman…" I was preparing to let him know exactly what I thought of his proposal assumptions when he suddenly produced a huge diamond ring out of thin air and lifted it into my line of sight.

Any further objections died in my mouth.

"Like I said." He smirked, taking my hand and sliding the ring on my finger. "You should probably put on your engagement ring before my parents get here."

My vision swam, and my lungs seized.

He'd proposed—kinda.

He wanted to be my husband again.

And I wanted to be his wife more than I'd ever wanted anything.

It might have taken us some time to figure it out.

But we'd fallen in love in less than a day.

Not even utter devastation and two years apart could erase that.

A love like ours wasn't measured in years, distance, or time apart.

It was never-ending.

An electrical current traveled through me, prickling the hairs on the back of my neck the same way it had the first time I'd laid eyes on him and then again that day at the police station.

Only, this time, I realized that it was the overwhelming sensation of *right*.

The diamond was gorgeous, but that feeling had less to do with the stone and more to do with the man who had given it to me.

He was right.

We were right.

We'd *always* been right.

So, with absolute certainty—and despite the fact that he hadn't asked—I laughed a throaty, "Yes."

His smile grew exponentially. Then he pressed his smiling mouth to mine and taunted, "See? I told you you'd say yes."

I slapped his arms and wiped a stray tear on my shoulder. "Don't be an ass right now. I'm too happy to give you any attitude."

"Okay, Elisabeth Leblanc—with an S and a lowercase B—I won't be an ass right now while you're feeling happy."

The familiar words turned the waterworks on full force. "God, don't be sweet, either. Just stand there and tell me you love me."

"I love you."

He did. I had not one single doubt about that.

I threw my arms around his neck, buried my face in his neck, and mumbled, "Never mind. That just made it worse."

His shoulders shook as he laughed, and he smoothed his hands up and down my back, his lips peppering kisses anywhere his mouth could reach.

It was then that I understood what he'd meant when he'd said that his lungs had inflated for the first time since he'd found me sitting on the couch the night I left.

Because, for the first time since I'd made the decision to leave, I took my first real breath. I clung to his shoulders and basked in the beauty of it all.

After a few minutes, he murmured, "Baby, you gotta let me go if I still need to go dig up some sweet potatoes."

I sniffled and sat up, staring down at my ring. "Nah. I think this will be enough to distract them from the lack of carbohydrates on the table."

"Probably." He grinned just as the front door swung wide open and Kristen sauntered in with Devon on her heels, carrying a huge tray of pies.

"Damn it, Kristen," Roman barked, shoving away from me and striding toward his sister. "He's a bodyguard, not a bellhop."

"Oh, shut up, Roman. He offered to help. Besides, he's going to be eating some of it, too." She batted her eyelashes. "I made extra since I'm sure a big, strong guy like Devon has quite an appetite." She bit her lip and shot Roman an exaggerated wink.

While Kristen did think Devon was hot (and he was), she really just enjoyed screwing with her brother.

"Oh, for fuck's sake," he bit out, snatching the tray from Devon's hands.

"Roman!" Cathy scolded as she came through the front door. "It's Thanksgiving. Can you give the cursing a rest?" Her hands were filled with a million bags, and a huge smile covered her face as her gaze met mine.

I hopped off the counter, straightened my dress, and headed to help her. I was pulling bags from her hands when I was wrapped in a hug from behind.

"My girl came home," Rome mumbled to himself before releasing me. Taking the bags from my hands, he grumbled at his wife, "Woman, I told you I'd get the bags."

"And I told you…" She kept talking, but I lost her words as she bustled to the kitchen.

As I watched the man I loved—who, only minutes earlier, had slipped a ring on my finger—as he argued with his sister in the kitchen, his parents chattering under their breath, and one lost and confused bodyguard skillfully trying to make his escape out the back door, I realized that

Rome was not wrong.
I was home.

CHAPTER TWENTY-TWO

ROMAN

"Shelly," I called to my secretary. "Where is the new offer from Wells?"

She peeked her head around the corner. "I'm assuming it's on the table with the rest of your mail. I didn't open anything that was personally addressed to you."

I groaned, cutting my eyes to the table that had to be moved into my office sometime over the last week, for no other purpose than to hold all of the mail I'd received while I'd been out.

I quietly cursed myself for having made the rule about mail after Shelly had opened a blow-up doll Kristen had sent to the office for my birthday. Only it hadn't been my birthday and she'd only done it because she was pissed and knew that my secretary opened all my mail. She'd ordered it on her cell phone while impatiently sitting in the chair across from the desk, waiting for me to get off a business call.

Taking two weeks off to spend time with Elisabeth had been amazing. Part of it had been spent working with attorneys to figure out the best course of action in getting custody of a child who I couldn't even prove was mine. However, the other part, where I'd gotten to know Elisabeth again and then convinced her to marry me again, had been worth every minute of coming back to mountains of work at the office.

Less than two seconds after walking into my office, I made the decision that I needed to hire someone to help me run things.

I'd worked a lot since starting Leblanc Industries, but now that I had Elisabeth back, I had no interest in spending eighteen hours a day away from her. It was time I started living again, and what better way than with the woman I loved at my side.

"Thanks, Shelly," I said, dismissing her and moving toward an only slightly smaller version of the Alps made out of unopened boxes and envelopes.

Twenty minutes later, I was still searching for a more-than-likely-shit offer from Wells when my hand landed on a padded envelope with no return address. I flipped it over to check the back, but besides my address and a postmark from nine days ago, it was completely blank.

Curious, I ripped the top off, slid the contents out, and then stopped breathing.

My entire body turned to granite when I realized what I was holding.

Two plastic baggies filled with four Q-tips each.

Another filled with curly, blond hairs.

Another with darker-blond locks.

And, finally, a toothbrush.

I frantically tore the two pieces of folded paper open.

One was a generic consent to DNA testing that had to have been printed off the Internet, but the only thing that mattered was that it had Tessa's name at the top and it had been signed by Clare Noir.

The second paper caused a heavy weight to sink in my stomach.

Hand-written on an otherwise blank piece of paper was a note that said:

Roman,

You were right. I should have gotten in the car. Unfortunately, you were wrong too. There's nothing that can be done to help me anymore, but I'm begging you to use this DNA and do what I can't.

Save Tessa. Get her as far away from Walt as you can, even if that means away from me too.

I wasn't sure exactly what you'd need, so I swabbed each of our mouths with the Q-tips. The toothbrush is Walt's.

All I ask is that, one day, when I'm gone, you'll remind her how much I loved her.

Please hurry.
-Clare

I felt like someone had kicked me in the stomach even as my mind celebrated the breakthrough.

That woman was handing me a child she loved.

My child.

Elisabeth's child

Clare's child.

Despite the fact that it meant losing her.

My stomach wrenched at such a selfless sacrifice.

My conscience exploded with guilt.

I couldn't leave her hanging in the breeze.

But I had no idea what the fuck I could do.

I slid the contents back in the envelope and marched over to my desk. Then I snatched the receiver up as I dragged my wallet from my pocket and found his card.

"Light," he growled in greeting.

"I just got a package in the mail from Clare Noir. A legal consent for testing, baggies full of possible DNA for her, Tessa, and Walter, and a letter begging me to save the girl."

Silence.

"Heath! Did you hear me?"

"Walt's DNA won't be admissible in court," he said, emotionless.

"Hers will though. And, if we can confirm that Tessa is Elisabeth's, that's all we need to prove foul play, right?"

He didn't answer my question. "You at the office?"

"Yeah."

"Hang tight. I'm on my way." Then he hung up.

Keeping the phone to my ear, I hit the button with my hand then released it and dialed again. "I need to speak with Detective Rorke immediately. It's an emergency."

After I'd relayed the story to him, he too stated that he was on his way over to my office then disconnected.

I debated calling Elisabeth, but I didn't want to get her hopes up. I had no fucking idea what the hell this meant for us. Yes, we now had the DNA, but I had a feeling getting custody of that little girl wasn't going to be an overnight process.

With restless legs, I spent the next fifteen minutes pacing my office as I reread the letter from Clare over and over again. Each time I finished, my anxiety and my resolve to help her grew stronger.

By the time Heath came striding through my door, I was roaring with adrenaline.

"Letter!" he demanded.

I handed it his way then fisted my hands on my hips and watched him read, recounting each word by memory as his eyes scanned the page. His jaw clenched, the muscles twitching as he ground his teeth.

I waited. And waited. And waited.

He had to have read it at least four times. But he never looked up.

"What are my options here?" I finally asked.

He said not a single word as he dropped the letter to the floor and headed right back out my door.

"Light," I called after him.

His long legs swallowed up the distance to the elevator as I marched after him.

"Where the fuck are you going? I need some help here."

His blue gaze swung to mine, causing me to flinch when I caught sight of the hollow orbs staring back at me. He shook his head, raked a hand through his hair, and boomed, "Fuck!" His fist slammed into the metal doors just before they slid open and revealed Rorke standing inside.

The air turned thick as the two men saw each other.

"You are not here," Heath said dangerously.

"Light," Rorke warned.

He took a giant step into the elevator, bumping his chest with Rorke's. "*You* are not *fucking* here!"

I caught the elevator door before it closed and climbed inside. "What the fuck is going on?" I rumbled, squeezing in front of Heath, who had passed the point of anger and was teetering precariously on the edge of blinding rage.

"This man just cost you your daughter," he growled.

My body jerked. "Excuse me?" I planted a hand on his chest and turned to face Rorke.

"I did not!" the detective assured, visibly shaken.

"You smoke your mole out yet?" Heath shot over my shoulder. "Because I guarantee Walter Noir has heard that his wife gave up DNA to the police and they are both probably dead or dying by now."

Rorke cocked his head to the side and spat, "I kept it quiet."

Heath turned and jabbed the L button, muttering under his breath, "If *you* know, it's not quiet enough."

My mind was spinning, and I couldn't keep up. Finally, I'd had enough. "Somebody tell me what the fuck is going on right fucking now!" I seethed in a volatile whisper.

Rorke started with, "Light thinks—"

He didn't get another word out before Heath dove around me, grabbed the front of his shirt, and slammed him up against the back of the elevator, snarling, "I *know*! I don't *think*! I fucking know! You have a goddamn cop feeding

Noir our every move. Now, once again, I have to figure out a way to clean up your mess."

"You're not cleaning up shit, Light. You go anywhere near that house, you'll blow the entire investigation."

"Fuck you. Fuck your department. Fuck your entire jacked-up investigation." He gave him another hard slam into the elevator. "I swear to God, Rorke. One fucking uniform follows me, I'll have your badge."

"Really? Because it sounds like you're about to lose yours." Rorke pushed back.

Heath's lips formed an angry snarl. "What's he gonna do? Call the cops?"

The elevator dinged, and the doors opened to the lobby. Heath stomped out but stopped only a few feet away to turn back and look at me. "You coming with me or what?"

I was. I so was.

Even though I had no idea what the hell was about to go down.

CHAPTER TWENTY-THREE

CLARE

It had been nine days since I'd mailed the DNA to Roman.

I hadn't heard anything back.

I didn't know if that was a good or a bad thing.

His face wasn't on the news as a missing person.

But the cops hadn't showed up to take my daughter yet, either.

I wasn't positive that was the way it would work, but every night as I fell asleep with her in my arms, a knife under my mattress, Walt curled up behind me, I had the sweetest dreams about that moment.

It would kill me to tell her goodbye.

But the relief of knowing she was finally out of his reach would make it all worth it.

It was the day after Thanksgiving, and I was decorating the house for Christmas when I heard Walt coming down the stairs.

Tessa froze when she heard him, but I gave her a smile and a wink and tossed her a few of the plastic ornaments I'd managed to untangle from the lights.

I kept my back to him, hoping he'd ignore me.

I'd never been more wrong.

I felt him get close, and I steeled myself for his usual hug and kiss.

Only, this time, I felt his hand wrap around my neck, cutting my air off, as he spun me and slammed my back against the wall.

My scream was unable to escape past his grip on my throat.

I had always been afraid of Walt, but I'd never, not once, seen him as angry as he was in that moment.

His face was nearly vibrating as he exploded. "You gave the police our DNA!"

That was it.

The time had come.

It was my day to die.

And, as my eyes frantically flashed to Tessa, who was screaming on the floor, my only thoughts were that I'd failed her for the first, and ultimately last, time.

ROMAN

"What are you planning to do?" I asked, sitting in the passenger's seat of Heath's white Explorer as he gunned it toward the Noir residence.

"Haven't made it that far," he grunted, swerving around

227

traffic.

Fuck. This does not sound good.

"Then maybe we should pull the fuck over and develop some sort of plan of action here," I argued.

He ignored me and lifted a phone to his ear. "It's Light. I need surveillance at Noir's temporarily shut off for about an hour." Pause. "Well, that's up to you, but there's about to be a fuck-ton of my face up in that shit." Pause. "Then that's on you. But I'd suggest you do it now." Pause. "Right. I've got Leblanc with me."

I heard the man on the other end of the phone shouting as Heath pulled the phone away and pressed the end button.

Fuck. That sounds even worse.

"Heath, man…I'm not sure about this. I want this done too, but I don't think this is the way to—"

He cut me off. "He's gonna kill her. If he hasn't already."

"Tessa?" I asked, my heart lurching into my throat.

He shook his head, keeping his eyes on the road. "*Clare.* Then he's gonna pack up your kid and leave the city. We might find him again." His haunting gaze flashed to mine. "But we might not. The one thing I can swear to you is that we do *not* have time to pull over and work out a plan of action. Now, I can pull over, drop you off, and you can walk away from all of this here and now. Or you can reach into my back seat, dig out my vest, put that motherfucker on, and follow me into the pits of Hell to retrieve your daughter."

I gritted my teeth.

It wasn't a choice at all.

If he was right, this might have been my only shot to bring her home to Elisabeth.

So I stayed silent, leaned into the back seat, and pulled a fucking *Kevlar* vest on, vowing to arm our boys in blue with Rubicon the first chance I got. And then I prepared to take back my family.

CLARE

"You stupid cunt!" Walt yelled into my face.

His hand was still around my throat, and I struggled to pry his fingers away.

I couldn't breathe, and I was precariously close to losing consciousness.

But knowing that, if I let go, I'd probably never wake up again gave me the strength to slam my knee into his groin.

His body jerked and his grip loosened long enough for me suck in a sweet gasp of oxygen.

He regained his hold on me, but with fresh air in my lungs and a lifetime of fear fueling me, I threw my fists into his face and another knee into his groin, and then I shoved him as hard as I could. Desperation made me strong, and he stumbled back.

Suddenly free, I took off at a dead sprint. Snatching Tessa off the floor and then darting to the front door.

My pulse was roaring in my ears, but I could hear his footsteps echoing behind me.

I pushed myself faster.

I struggled with the door before swinging it open and racing out front.

I only made it two steps before pain detonated at the

back my head, forcing me to a sharp halt before snatching me backward.

"No!" I screamed as Tessa fell from my arms.

ROMAN

Heath parked one street over, and we jogged the rest of the way up to the Noirs' front gate. His gun was drawn as he scanned the perimeter. The sun was just starting to set, and the pink Georgia sky made for a picturesque view. From the outside, it looked just like any other Atlanta mansion. No one could have imagined the evil residing inside.

However, as a man's vicious yell came from inside the house, I jolted into a reality I'd never wanted to be a part of.

"Fuck!" Heath growled. "I'm going around the side to see if I can get in. You stay here," he ordered before bolting away.

The man yelled again, and this time, I heard the shrill of a child screaming too. An icy rage sent a shiver down my back, and fire shot through my veins. Shaking the tall, metal structure, I furiously tried to find a way inside. The steel wouldn't budge no matter how hard I fought. Refusing to stop until I got to Tessa, I attempted to squeeze my bulky body between the bars, but it was useless.

"Fuck. Fuck. Fuck!" I snarled, using my weight to try to pry the bars apart.

I'd managed to wedge my shoulder between two of them when I saw the front door swing open. Clare came flying out, Tessa in her arms, Walter Noir directly behind her.

"Clare!" I yelled as Walter snatched the back of her hair, pulling her to an abrupt halt and sending Tessa to the ground.

"No!" Clare screamed as she fell.

I shoved an arm through the bars, frantically trying to reach her, but she was yards away. "Tessa!" I shouted next, hoping I could get her to come to me. Her small body would have fit through the bars.

Terror churned in my gut as Walter slammed Clare into the ground then charged after the child.

I rammed my shoulder into the gate again, yelling, "Don't you fucking touch her!"

I swear to God I was going to rip that son of a bitch in half.

If *only* I could get my hands on him.

CLARE

I twisted, diving for Walt's ankle as he went after Tessa. I caught him with one hand and sent him stumbling to the ground just as I heard a man yelling. I glanced up, fear consuming me at the possibility of it being one of Walt's men.

Only for my heart to burst when I saw Roman Leblanc standing like a white knight coming to rescue Tessa from the dragon's lair.

He was there.

Someone had come.

The sob tore through me as I fought to keep Walt down. "Take her!" I shrieked. "Take her!"

"I can't reach her!" he shouted, thrusting his arm through the metal bars of my prison.

Walt reached back, ripping my hand off his leg.

"Tessa, go!" I screamed when he got back to his feet.

She was hysterical, tears streaming down her face, blood dripping from her scraped knees and elbows.

"Mama!" she cried, running from Walt but too afraid to go to Roman.

She was so close to being free. I couldn't allow him to get his hands on her again. Drawing up the remainder of my strength, I pushed to my feet and sprinted after him. Slamming into his back, I once again took him to the ground.

"Goddamn it!" he barked, rolling over, his fists flying at my face.

"Tessa, go!" I ordered, doing my best to defend myself from Walt's blows.

Even through the struggle, I heard Roman trying to coax her over to him.

"Tessa, don't you fucking move!" Walt barked, his hands momentarily slowing their assault.

I couldn't see her from my position, but I prayed that Walt's reaction meant she was heading to Roman.

I couldn't do anything but hurry her along and try to ease her into the arms of a stranger. "Tessa, it's okay. Please, baby, go to him."

Then, suddenly, the chaos stopped.

Everyone stopped yelling.

Tessa's cries fell quiet.

And, in the silence, I actually heard the Earth begin spinning again.

She had to have gone to Roman.

He had to have finally gotten her.

She was safe.

She was safe.

Oh my God. She's finally safe.

Tears poured from my eyes.

My job was done, and within a second, my entire battered, beaten, and exhausted body finally gave out. Gravity finally defeated me as I sagged on the concrete driveway.

My arms and legs were limp as one more of Walt's fists landed on my face, but I didn't feel it amongst the euphoria and relief.

"She's safe," I found myself repeating as I felt Walt rise up off me.

Keeping my eyes closed, I waited for the final blow that would end it all.

I smiled, eager for the darkness.

But it never came.

The familiar sound of my name made my eyes flutter open.

Walt was standing there. A gun to his temple.

A long, muscular arm at the other end of the trigger. My daughter safely tucked into his side. Warm, blue eyes I immediately recognized stared back at me.

"Heath, give me the girl!" Roman called.

Heath?

I blinked as he dug the gun into Walt's temple. Then he whispered something in Tessa's ear and set her down.

Glancing back at me over her shoulder, she reluctantly ran to Roman and clung to his neck as he gently guided her between the bars of the gate.

"Just get her out of here," I begged.

"Oh, I am, but I'm taking you, too," he said.

Oh my God. It has to be a dream.

But not even my mind could have conjured a moment that beautiful.

"Okay, Luke," I whispered.

The story continues with
Heath Light and Clare Noir in

TRANSFER

Coming September 27, 2016

I fell in love with a man who didn't exist.

What started out as romance ended in hell.
His words turned to razor blades.
His kisses converted to fists.
His embrace became my cage.
His body transformed into a weapon, stealing parts of me
until ultimately….
I broke.

I hated him.
My sole job in life became to protect our daughter.

I wasn't sure I'd ever escape the prison he'd skillfully crafted
from my fears.
Until the day our savior arrived.

This is the story of how I escaped the man who thought he
owned me.
The *transfer* of my *life* and my *family*.

OTHER BOOKS

ABOUT THE AUTHOR

Born and raised in Savannah, Georgia, Aly Martinez is a stay-at-home mom to four crazy kids under the age of five, including a set of twins. Currently living in South Carolina, she passes what little free time she has reading anything and everything she can get her hands on, preferably with a glass of wine at her side.

After some encouragement from her friends, Aly decided to add "Author" to her ever-growing list of job titles. So grab a glass of Chardonnay, or a bottle if you're hanging out with Aly, and join her aboard the crazy train she calls life.

Facebook: www.facebook.com/AuthorAlyMartinez
Twitter: twitter.com/AlyMartinezAuth
Goodreads: www.goodreads.com/AlyMartinez

55656777R10141

Made in the USA
Lexington, KY
29 September 2016